# Pulp

Vol. 2

MW00475208

**Andrew Bourelle**

**"Doc" Clancy**

**Timothy Friend**

**Adam S. Furman**

**Nils Gilbertson**

**Peter W.J. Hayes**

**Serena Jayne**

**Mandi Jourdan**

**Victoria Weisfeld**

Edited by Alec Cizak
Uncle B. Publications

Pulp Modern Vol. 2 No. 5  Summer 2020
Published and produced by
Uncle B. Publications and Larque Press LLC
Pulp Modern is funded in part by Yuan Sang

Chief Editor: Alec Cizak
Design: Richard Krauss
Illustrator: Ran Scott
Cover: Rick McCollum for "Ghost Town"
Cartoons: Bob Vojtko (p 41, 69, 83)

Printed on demand from June 2020

Printed in the United States of America and other countries.

Contact information for Uncle B. Publications may be obtained through the
website: pulp-modern.blogspot.com
Contact information for Larque Press LLC may be obtained through the
website: larquepress.com

ISBN-13: 978-1-7342177-1-1

# PM5 CONTENTS

Interior artwork by Ran Scott

# From the Editor

## Alec Cizak

WELL, DEAR READERS, here we are at the cutting edge of all we once knew. A pandemic any fool could have predicted has locked down the world. Those of us who don't risk our lives attempting to save the most vulnerable sit in our houses, our apartments, our trailers, wherever we call home, and wonder whether the world will return to a façade of normal before we lose our individual minds. This is the disaster every realist has predicted for decades, the crisis the lazy have been craving, the excuse our world leaders have sought in order to sweep away those pesky civil liberties we enjoy in the West (well, *once* enjoyed). This is not to say the stay-at-home order isn't necessary. It is. But let's be honest, the paranoid, the germaphobes, the individualists, they've all been proven correct. The so-called conspiracy theorists must be soiling themselves with simultaneous delight and terror. Standing in line for consumer goods, once a folly of the Soviet Union, will now be standard routine around the world.

How much longer will independent fiction survive in a world eager to embrace an international police state? Well, friends and lovers, *Pulp Modern* has survived multiple assassination attempts. If the writers and readers are game, we editors will continue doing our part.

We kick off this issue with an all-too appropriate tale of life after the apocalypse. We move from there to a crime tale puncturing civility's thin veneer. We head into the future after that and then return to the past for a good vs. evil struggle in the American Southwest. Two nasty little crime stories follow before we launch into another tale of good and evil and redemption. We close out this issue with a pair of quiet, refined crime stories.

As always, I thank you, the reader, for whom all these efforts are made. Stay safe, stay healthy. We have many more miles to travel.

*Survival is a selfish endeavor.*

# Companion
## Andrew Bourelle

THE BOY AND his dog approached the farmhouse, the boy holding his shotgun, the dog padding along beside him. The sun was low, and if they didn't find anything to eat here, the boy was afraid he was going to kill the dog and eat it.

In the front yard was an old water pump, and the boy jacked the handle a dozen times before coffee-colored liquid burst out. He let the water run, hoping it would turn clear. His mouth was dry and full of sores. His stomach ached and it was difficult to stand upright from the pain. His head throbbed and he found it hard to see clearly.

At the door, he sloughed off his backpack, which was small and once carried his textbooks through the halls of junior high school. He dug his hands in past a sheath knife, a can opener, spare batteries, Band-Aids, and a few *Wolverine* comic books. Finally, he found his flashlight.

The door was unlocked, and it swung open silently.

The dog—a young rust-spotted coonhound—went in ahead, its head low, sniffing. The boy followed. He resisted the temptation to rummage through the cupboards and made himself do a sweep of the house first.

There was enough window-light in the foyer and living room to see, but the hallway to the back of the house was dark. He found a child's bedroom, barely lit from the window. He swept the flashlight beam through the room and saw stuffed *Toy Story* characters, a shelf full of picture books, a child's drawing easel. Instead of being covered in crayon illustrations, the sheet of paper contained a jaggedly scrawled message:

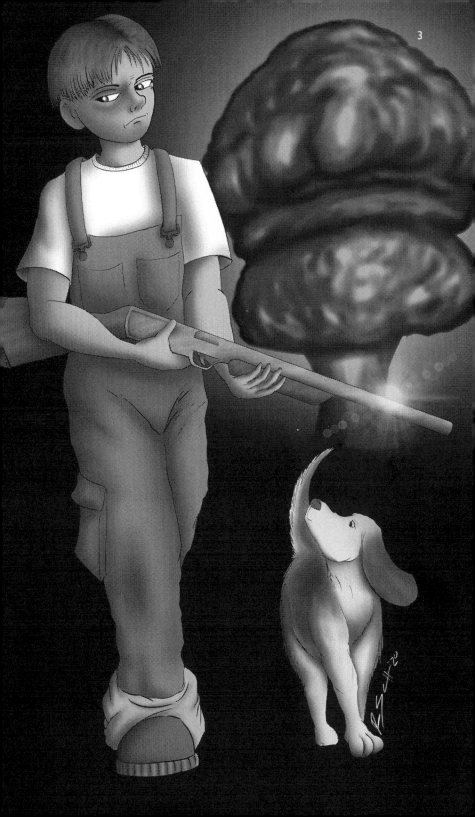

WITHOUT SOMEONE TO LOVE,
WHAT IS THE POINT OF GOING ON?

The boy stared at the message, thinking. After he and his mom had heard the sound —like reality itself splitting open— they watched from their front yard as the cloud pillared into the sky, turning into a gray stalk of cauliflower as tall as a mountain and pulsing with red and purple flame. The explosion was far away, but warm air pushed against them like heat from an open oven door.

He felt some nausea those first few weeks, fatigue and headaches. No appetite. But that was all. His mom's hair fell out in clumps. She threw her food up undigested or it came out as oily diarrhea. Toward the end, she begged him to shoot her with his father's shotgun. She was a skeleton with skin, and because her nose wouldn't stop bleeding, she wore a goatee of red crust. He wanted to hold her hand and help her through it, but he couldn't watch, couldn't listen. He went for a long walk during the night, and when he came home at dawn, he found her corpse rigid, buzzing with flies. Two feet of her intestine had slithered out of her rectum like a giant red worm.

As he buried her in the yard, he vowed it would be the last time he cried. But it wasn't. He cried through the winter. He ate the last stores of food, shot prairie rabbits or whitetail deer when he could. In the spring, he left home. He'd considered going in the direction of the city to look for his father, but that's where the cloud had risen and he wanted to believe his father was one of the lucky ones incinerated instantly. He went the other direction, into plains of rotten, unplowed crops.

In that first year, he encountered plenty of people. Some were hospitable and pitied a boy his age traveling alone.

Others weren't friendly, and he learned to use his shotgun for more than hunting.

When the dog started following him, it had been weeks since he'd seen another human. He left scraps of food for it, and after a few days, it approached and licked the juice from an empty tuna tin he held in his hand. That was in the spring when supplies were plentiful. Now it was summer and both he and the dog were starving.

The dog nudged him out of his stupor. He tore his eyes from the crayon message and patted the dog. It pressed its hot, dry nose against his hand.

He searched the rest of the house and found no people. And no food. The cabinet doors were open and cleanly scavenged. Even the spice containers were gone or emptied.

The gas appeared to be working—he could get a flame on the stove.

He went back outside to find the pump water had cleared. Icy liquid filled his cheeks and he gulped it down, vomited, and gulped down more. The dog lapped water from the puddle until its belly looked pregnant.

The boy shut off the water and sat in dry grass away from the pump. The dog pressed its bony fence-post ribs against his leg, and he scratched the animal behind the ears. The sky was darkening every second, and the boy knew that it would be easier to kill the dog in daylight. He would need to disembowel it. And then skin it. And then peel what little meat there was from the bones and put it in water to boil.

He wanted the liquid in his stomach to be enough, but as he ran his hands over the dog's prickly coat, his mouth was discharging saliva he couldn't control.

After the sun set, he walked through darkness into the child's room, sat on the toddler bed, shined his flashlight on the message written on the easel. He hugged the dog and let it pant hot breath against his tear-streaked face. He turned off the flashlight and let the orange glow disappear from the window.

He thought about the other option: allowing the dog to eat instead.

He was afraid the sound of the gun would scare the dog, or perhaps it would have some qualms about eating the person who had taken care of it.

He curled into a fetal ball on the tiny bed, and the dog snuggled against him. He would try to sleep and decide what to do in the daylight.

HE AWOKE TO the dog's barking. He gripped its fur instinctively and held it back. A flashlight shone on them, blinding him. The dog snarled and pulled against him, but he kept his grip on it.

"I got a gun," a female voice said.

Not a woman. A girl's voice, raspy but distinctly young.

"If that dog bites me," she said, "I'm putting a bullet in its head and another one in yours."

"Shhh," the boy said to the dog, stroking its fur. "It's okay." Then, to the girl, he said, "Turn off the light."

"Toss your shotgun over in the corner."

Still holding the dog with one hand, he threw the gun into a pile of stuffed animals, the barrel pointed away from him.

"Let him sniff you," the boy said.

He wrapped both hands around the dog—it didn't have a collar—and inched toward the light. The girl turned out the light, and they were enveloped in blackness.

"I swear to God," the girl said, "if that thing bites me . . ."

She trailed off. The dog started sniffing the way dogs do when they're being introduced to someone new. The boy felt the tension in its muscles relaxing. He eased up on his hold. He heard the dog licking.

"All right, all right," she said. "That's enough."

The boy's eyes had adjusted enough to notice a glimmer of pale blue light coming in through the window. The sun was rising. They'd slept most of the night.

The girl—just a shape in the gray light—pushed past him and grabbed his shotgun.

"What are you doing here?" she asked.

"Looking for food. Do you have any?"

"No," she said, "but you do."

SHE HELD THE shotgun on him and walked him and the dog out of the house and into the front yard, where they could see better. He lifted a lawn chair that was lying on its side and set it upright. Then he found another and did the same. He sat and gestured for her to sit in the other chair.

She did. She kept the shotgun generally pointed in his direction. He saw that her other weapon was a revolver strapped to her hip like a cowboy.

The dog settled in next to the boy's chair, dropping its head down to the dead grass but keeping its eyes on the girl.

Every second the air was lightening. The girl had a tangled shock of red hair and a smattering of acne on her cheeks. She wasn't beautiful, but he figured that in the old world, if he'd seen her in school, with her hair properly brushed and some makeup on, he would have thought she was cute. She was older than him by a few years.

"Do you live here?" the boy said.

"No," she said. "I live close by. The best time to hunt is at sunrise. I was walking by and saw the door hanging open. I knew that was different."

"There's water here," the boy said, trying to be helpful, friendly.

"I got water," the girl said. "My well's working just like this one."

"Oh," the boy said.

He was thirsty and wanted to walk out into the yard and take another drink, try to drown the hunger pangs in his belly. He didn't think she was going to shoot him, but he didn't want to provoke her.

She asked where he was from, and he told her, and she said she'd been there once when her high school played his in football.

"I was a cheerleader," she said.

They were both silent after that, thinking about how the world had changed.

The girl balanced the shotgun in her lap and brought her arms up to work on her hair. She was piling the wild strands on top of her head and securing them there with a clip. There was enough light now to see her clearly. Her cheeks were sunken in, and her neck looked very thin. With her hair up, her head looked like a bird skull perched on a twig. Her shirtsleeves slid down to her elbows, revealing toothpick arms.

Despite how thin she was, she looked cuter in the light. He could picture her—stronger, healthier—on the sidelines of a football field in her cheerleading outfit. He imagined her doing a cartwheel, exposing her legs and colored undershorts.

"So what are we going to do about this dog?" she said as she finished clipping her hair in place.

"If you want to eat him," the boy said, "you'll have to shoot me first."

"I was afraid you'd say that."

She took a deep breath, and for a moment he thought she was steeling herself for doing just that. Instead, she said, "Well, I better go hunting then. The best time for deer is in the morning. I haven't seen one in a while, but maybe today's the day." She hefted the shotgun. "I'm going to borrow this."

"I'll go," the boy said. He felt a burst of energy—a survival instinct telling him what to do. "You stay here. I'll bring something back."

She thought about it.

"Okay," she said.

"My house is two down that way," she said, pointing. "Come find me there."

The boy walked into the rising warmth of sunset, and the dog followed. He considered running—going as far as he could from the house. But he was too weak to make it very far. And he thought she might make a good companion if he could just feed her, take her mind off the dog.

BY MID-MORNING, he hadn't seen anything. He knew his best chance now was a rabbit, so he replaced the double-aught buck in his shotgun with birdshot. He found a wide expanse of overgrown grasses and began stomping through it. The dog went ahead of him, its head down, sniffing, and its tail wagging. It was hard work, just walking, and the boy felt lightheaded.

He caught a blur of movement and turned his head in time to see a coyote slipping into a copse of trees. He pulled the gun up, but it was too late. He didn't think the birdshot would kill it at this distance anyway.

The dog hadn't spotted it.

They crept over to the trees, but he couldn't find the coyote anywhere. The dog seemed to catch its scent, but it led him to a field where the coyote was nowhere in sight.

"Dammit," the boy said, taking a fistful of his hair and yanking on it, trying to clear his head. He wanted to cry. That might have been his only chance.

The dog started barking.

A feral cat with wild, clumpy hair was stepping along a fence rail about twenty yards away. It arched its back and prepared to hop down and skitter away. The boy had only a second. He brought the shotgun up and blinked his eyes when it kicked against his shoulder. In the instant his eyes were closed, the cat disappeared.

The dog ran forward and the boy waited, hoping.

When the dog came back dragging the limp cat in its mouth, relief flooded through him like the effects of a drug.

He'd just saved all their lives.

THE GIRL WENT to work on the cat immediately. He'd field dressed it, but she took it from there. Using his knife, she sliced the fur down the inside of its legs and cut circles around its paws. Then she pulled the fur and it slid off the legs, down its torso, and finally its front legs. As the hide came off, it made a peeling sound, like she was pulling a strand of masking tape off a roll. The fur remained attached at the neck, an inside-out tee shirt that couldn't quite fit over the head. The girl used a long serrated bread knife to saw through the spine and remove the cat's head. She tossed the inside-out hide into the sink with the head still attached. Without its hair, the cat looked like a tiny, headless human.

She put it in water to boil.

She was giddy, smiling. They both were excited. The guns sat on the table, forgotten. She showed him the house. In the living room, she'd set up a cluster of candles next to the couch and a shelf of paperback books. After dark, she said, she liked to sit and read. She'd brought a mattress out and laid it in front of the fireplace. It was a big house, but she'd only made this room her own.

When the cat was cooked, he expected them to tear into it. But she set the table and had him go outside and fill up water cups. They sat down to eat like civilized people. They picked as much gray-boiled meat off the cat as they could while the dog paced on the floor, ropes of saliva stretching from its mouth.

"Okay," she said to the dog, "you can have the rest."

She carried the platter with the carcass to the front porch. She set it down and the dog went after it, crunching the bones in its teeth.

"Come on," the girl said conspiratorially, closing the door and leaving the dog outside.

She grabbed the boy's hand and pulled him down the hall to one of the bedrooms. She thrust her body against his and kissed him. He tasted the grease of the cat meat on her lips. She pushed him down on the bed and tugged his jeans down, and as she climbed on top of him, he thought, *Is this really happening?*

THEY BATHED IN the cold water from her well, giggling. He built a fire even though they didn't need it, and they lay naked on the mattress in front of it. The dog stretched out on the floor next to them, resting its chin on its paws, and fell asleep and snored. Its jowls fluttered with each loud exhalation.

The girl propped herself on an elbow and told the boy about her life before. The boy spoke about anything he could think of. He had spoken so little for so long that soon his voice was hoarse. He stared at the girl, the firelight dancing on her skin, and thought about how much life can change in only a day.

HE AWOKE TO find her getting dressed.

"I'm going hunting," she whispered. "Go back to sleep."

There was a hint of blue morning light in the windows.

"I'll go," he said, rising.

"You're sweet," she said, and kissed him. "Bring something

back so we have the strength to make love again."

He liked how she said it: *make love*.

The dog didn't wake. He watched its chest rise and fall, and decided to let it sleep.

HIS MIND WANDERED as he walked. Two days ago, he had been thinking of killing himself. Today, he was thinking about the freckles on her chest and shoulders, the way her face looked in the firelight as she smiled and told him what her favorite movies had been.

A mile from the house, he found tracks in a dirt lot. They might have been dogs, but he thought they were probably coyotes. He didn't know enough about tracking animals to know how fresh they were, but he looked around and debated. He saw a rabbit burst from a clump of brush. He swung the shotgun up, but the rabbit was hidden before he could draw a bead on it.

Still, he'd seen where it had gone. He stepped forward, the gun ready, hoping to flush it out and shoot it on the run. His heart accelerated and he tried to control his breathing.

*This is important*, he thought. *So much is depending on—*

A gunshot rang out from far away. It echoed from the direction he'd come. He froze, his legs suddenly weak.

He started running.

HE FOUND THEM in the front yard. She had positioned the dog on its back and was disemboweling it like she was field-dressing a deer. When she saw him approaching, she rose. Her arms were bloodied to the elbows. The pistol was lying in the grass a few feet away.

"Don't overreact," she said, holding out a red-painted hand. "We need more to eat than an anorexic cat."

He looked at the dog, its body as flaccid as the cat after he'd shot it. Its head was upside down in a swamp of blood. The dog's tongue was hanging out between the teeth of its relaxed jaws. She'd shot it in the skull. At least it had been quick.

But the boy couldn't get enough air into his lungs.

"Go back out," the girl said, her voice calm. "I'll take care of everything. We'll have a nice big meal today. I'll smoke the rest and make jerky. We'll eat for a week. It will give us the strength to hunt, to find a way to plant some vegetables. This is the fresh start we need. I did it for *us*."

Her face seemed genuinely concerned — apologetic. It was the face of a parent teaching a hard lesson to a child. *I know it hurts, but it has to be this way.*

He turned away and walked out to the road.

This was the world he lived in. It asked you to cross lines you never thought you would have to cross. But which lines would you cross and which ones would you refuse to go over, no matter what?

He ejected the birdshot from his shotgun. He loaded it with double-aught buck.

When he came back, her hands were in the viscera pile. She pulled out the heart and held it in her blood-slicked hands, inspecting it.

When she noticed him, she looked up and said, "We can eat th—"

The blast knocked her off her haunches and onto her back.

He stood over her. Blood gurgled out of her mouth, and she clutched at the holes in her neck and chest, trickling blood. She had a look on her face of surprise and sadness. Like her team had just lost a football game it was supposed to win.

He pointed the gun at her face, but stopped before pulling the trigger.

She was gone.

He staggered away from the house, fell onto his hands and knees. Dry-heaved. Ran and stumbled and fell and rose again.

He found the house where he'd met her and crawled into the child's bed where he and the dog had slept. He stared at the message on the easel. He curled in a fetal ball and lay there, drifting in and out of consciousness.

He wanted to cry but there were no more tears.

HE AWOKE IN darkness to the singing of coyotes. He could tell where the sound was coming from. They were with the bodies of the girl and the dog, singing to celebrate their feast.

The boy's stomach rumbled. His mouth started to water.

He could kill the coyotes and eat, but it felt wrong, like he was using the things he loved for bait. And he told himself he didn't care about feeding himself. Not anymore.

He wanted to feed the girl.

He wanted to feed the dog.

He wanted them back. But there wasn't any way to bring them back. No way to rewind the shot back into the gun, the missile back into the silo.

He fought the rage inside him for a long time, but as the coyotes' howls grew louder, he finally rose to his feet and walked in darkness toward their frenzied calls.

He shot two before the others ran off.

This time, he didn't bother with cooking. He just clambered for the knife in the darkness and crawled around in the smell of blood and gun smoke, hacking off slivers of flesh and shoving them into his mouth without regard for which body they came from.

**Andrew Bourelle** is the author of the novel *Heavy Metal* and coauthor with James Patterson of *Texas Ranger* and *Texas Outlaw*. His short stories have been published widely in literary journals and fiction anthologies, including *The Best American Mystery Stories*..

PULP MODERN

pulp-modern.blogspot.com

*Chinese proverb: A patient woman can
roast an ox with a lantern.*

# The Bowie Knife

## Peter W. J. Hayes

WHEN HE FIRST entered the shop, I was struck by his
physique and sense of style: his back straight as a plumb line
and shoulders thrown back, his head topped by an oiled black
pompadour as high as his forehead. His green gabardine suit
sported rakishly-angled side pockets, but was cut to his body
before twenty pounds rounded his belly like a radar dome. I
doubt he was more than five feet six, and with each step he
pushed up on his toes to look taller—a trick common among
men of his height.

I apologize for the detail, but in my business, it matters.
After almost forty years selling antiques throughout Texas,
I've learned it's just as important to understand the buyer
as the item being sold. From his black hair and olive skin I
knew his ancestors were Mexican, but that wasn't important.
I was looking for the swagger born of the confidence—and
willingness—to drop fifteen thousand dollars on a Hopi vase
or a frontier chest of drawers.

That particular tell didn't appear in the man's gait, but
another did. As he bobbed toward me, he ignored the
showroom and display items.

He was here to sell something.

"Good afternoon," he said, stopping in front of me.

"Good afternoon," I replied. "Is there something I can help
you with?"

"I am Etienne Garcia Busto." Despite looking up at me, his
eyes retained a haughtiness.

I smiled and nodded. The name meant nothing to me,
although time and a little research would reveal quite a bit.

But this was a tricky moment. He clearly expected recognition, and I didn't want to offend him.

"From Veracruz?"

The voice came from my right. Libby rose from the table where, perhaps, in 1841, John Neely Bryan signed the documents creating Dallas County, creating the city of Dallas.

An aside, if I may.

I'd acquired the table several years earlier. It had generated little interest, but I was confident it would sell. It was, after all, the perfect punch line. People who buy antiques want a story to tell, and the right buyer would understand how that rough and unassuming table was the perfect ending to any conversation about how far and fast Dallas had grown.

Libby circled next to me. She was my height, slim, with a physique men notice, or more accurately, can't miss. She dressed to be sure of that. She presented Mr. Busto her hand. He bowed, took her hand and gave the back of it a gentle kiss.

I noted that his pompadour efficiently hid a bald spot on the crown of his head. He straightened; his brown eyes warm. Libby graciously retrieved her hand.

"It is a pleasure to meet a woman of your…stature, and grace."

I wondered where he dragged the words from. I'd known Libby since the days when she tagged behind her father as he held estate sales and called auctions throughout Texas. In those days she was all bony legs, skinny forearms and scabbed knees, usually tucked in a corner watching us work.

Again, I must digress.

Her father and I were close—high school best friends who shared a string of firsts during our sophomore and junior years. First beers. First whiskey. First car accident (a surprisingly predictable sequence). Plus, a midnight visit to a rival high school during the football playoffs. That involved a kicked-in front door, spray paint, and a hog, plus an overnight stay with the Fort Worth police. We were introduced to handcuffs, fingerprinting, holding tanks and several hundred hours of community service.

But Wayne and I returned to school heroes.

Within a week we both lost our virginity to Sue Donaldson, a bleach blonde who lived with her mother in a tornado-target of a trailer park. My own first experience lasted about as long as a sneeze. I remember Sue's mouth tasted of cherry gum, which she never stopped chewing throughout the entire experience. Eighteen years later, she and Wayne divorced their respective spouses, married, and ten months later Libby was born.

It's a funny old world.

I apologize. Perhaps Libby is right…I *do* digress too much.

"The Bustos of Veracruz are direct descendants of General Santa Anna," Libby said huskily, obviously repeating herself. Something unsaid asked me to clarify if I was deaf, dumb or just slow.

I turned to Mr. Busto, straightened and offered my hand. "My apologies, Mr. Busto, I should have recognized someone of your eminence—and importance—to the histories of our two countries. Unfortunately, I am not as young as I used to be."

He hesitated, apparently torn between magnanimity and storming out of the shop. Noblesse oblige won out.

"It is a tiny thing, Mr…?"

"Farrow. I am the proprietor of this small and dusty establishment."

He smiled, in the way of people used to the false modesty of politicians and, apparently, owners of antique shops. He took in the showroom with a practiced eye.

"Not so small, and not so dusty, I believe."

"You are very kind."

I sensed Libby's restlessness. She wanted us to get on with it, but I learned many years ago to slow down with anyone who might be a big fish.

"And I believe you are honest." Busto smiled, and now it was my turn to be reminded of politicians and, well, used car salesmen.

"Libby and I do our best." I wanted to include Libby in the conversation, because I guessed part of his decision to stay involved Libby's, shall we say, qualities.

"Of course." He glanced at Libby, his eyes never rising above her chest. Although, in fairness to him, that just meant his gaze stayed level.

"Perhaps I could help you in some way?" Libby asked. Her voice was an impressive mix of business briskness and subtle suggestion. The fact she could meld them so effortlessly left my mouth dry.

"It is a small thing." He hesitated.

"Perhaps for you, but I am certain most people would consider it very important." I couldn't leaven my words with Libby's sexuality, but I could certainly flatter.

He let the silence rage a few moments longer, then leaned toward us. "There is a family item I would like to make available. Perhaps, how do you say, test the market, if you understand my idea? Our family has held it for many years. It has been passed down. But perhaps the time is right to return it to its rightful home."

"We'd be more than glad to help, if we can." I smiled. "Do you have it with you? A photo perhaps?"

"Yes. Good." He straightened. "A photograph." He fumbled with his phone and tapped and swiped. A moment later he showed us the screen. "My ancestor General Antonio Lopez de Santa Anna acquired it. During the Battle of the Alamo. He always said it belonged to one of the American commanders. Your Jim Bowie."

The photo showed a knife with an oversized blade, crude brass hand guard and stained handle.

"Jim Bowie's knife?" Libby's voice was thick. She breathed out in a way that thrilled parts of me dormant since the death of my wife.

"As I said, perhaps it is time to return it to your country."

I regrouped. Despite being shown a photo of what might be the holy grail of Texas antiquing, there were practicalities, and I needed to be sure Libby understood them. "If I may, Mr. Busto, I would like to ask a few questions."

"Of course." The phone vanished into his pocket. "I would expect nothing less."

"If you say the knife comes from General Santa Anna, of

course it is authentic and your provenance is indisputable, but the marketplace will demand proof. We will need the verdict of an expert." I smiled in an attempt to lighten the blow. "I apologize."

He gave me the tedious look parents reserve for children struggling with homework.

"That said," I added quickly, "we would be happy to test the market for you. But perhaps, with something of this magnitude, you might want an established auction house. Heritage Auctions in Dallas, I could suggest, or even Sotheby's. There are collectors around the world willing to bid on this item. Their excitement might be…advantageous to you."

He waved his hand. "Mr. Farrow, I have great confidence in you. You have been in business for many years. Your reputation is impeccable. And I should say, this is less about the money than returning the knife to Texas. Where it belongs." He smiled, spread his hands, and for the first time I didn't see anything affected or insincere in his smile.

"We would be more than happy to explore the market for you," Libby cut in, recovering her voice. She bumped me with her hip, a message to keep Mr. Busto's sale with us.

"Yes," I soldiered on, "but one last question. There must be a large number of Busto descendants. I wonder if they are all in agreement about selling such an item?"

The vibration from Libby was so strong I thought she might explode. However, this was something she needed to know. Brokered sales are complicated. People use them to hide assets in the face of divorce, or to steal from an aging relative before the executor takes over. Lawsuits from ex-wives and family members often arrive in their wake. She needed to know the risk.

"It is something our family has discussed many times." Busto's tone was apologetic. "You must understand. Often, our family is asked if we own this artifact, and many times we say no. If it became known we own it, the pressure to donate it to a museum would be large. But my father passed away recently, and as the oldest son and executor of my father's estate, it is up to me to decide on its disposition. I can provide the legal documents to support this."

"That would be very helpful. Thank you." Beside me, Libby let out a long breath. "Of course," I added. "Given the circumstances, I agree about a private sale. Perhaps something with a collector we know well. Someone discreet?"

Busto's smile almost reached his ears. "You see, Mr. Farrow, I knew you would understand. Yes. I believe our family would truly appreciate such a transaction."

And that was that. Busto promised to return the next day with the knife.

The door barely slammed before Libby grabbed my arm and shrieked, "Holy crap! The Bowie knife!" Her face was flushed along the cheekbones, her eyes glittering.

One step at a time." I tried to be businesslike. "We'll need to verify the knife was made at the right time and check his papers, make sure that he has the right to sell it. But if all that holds, we've got the provenance."

Libby couldn't contain herself. She danced from behind the counter and did a little jig, almost knocking over a dome mantel clock that once—possibly—belonged to Juan Tejano. The way all the different parts of her moved was something to see. She slammed both hands down on the counter. "We can't do this as a private sale! We need to get people bidding. We can make thousands." Her eyes were hot in a way I hadn't seen before. "Maybe hundreds of thousands."

"No," I said. "This is exactly the sale we keep quiet. We want to build trust and word-of-mouth with our top clients, keep them coming back. You can't advertise your way into that kind of franchise."

Libby's eyes flared. "How can you think that way? We found the knife! We'll be the hottest shop in the state. Maybe the whole west!"

I raised my palms toward her. "Okay, okay. I'll think about it. But let's get it authenticated first. Make sure this isn't a scam." I chose not to remind her that we hadn't found the knife, the knife found us in the person of Etienne Busto.

"Sure." She tossed off the word, and I knew she had no

intention of listening to me. She never did. We'd been at odds since I took her in, and honestly, it was beginning to grate. I'd done her a favor and tried to teach her the business, but my comments always fell on deaf ears.

I apologize, but another digression is required.

As I mentioned, for years, Libby's father and I were best friends. Because of our similar business interests, before each auction he always invited me to review his inventory. If I spotted something a client wanted, or I liked, we'd agree on a price. In this way I built a serviceable business and we both learned what excited buyers.

He died from a heart attack immediately after a dusty three-hour auction on a hacienda just south of Amarillo. The timing was fortunate for me. My business was struggling and I owed Libby's father a substantial amount of money. It was terrible for Libby. She was fifteen and just beginning to blossom into the woman I know today. A year later, Libby's mother remarried. Six months after that Libby was arrested for stabbing her stepfather. Because of Libby's age, the trial was closed door and the court documents sealed. However, the judge, a good client of mine who collects Texas frontier memorabilia, told me about it one night over several glasses of bourbon. Apparently, when Libby was asked why she stabbed her stepfather, she described how the man visited her bed one night, and she stabbed him 'so he'd get I wasn't my mother.' Or so she put it.

The judge, whose grandfather was a Texas Ranger in the days when they alone were the law, sentenced Libby to four years for aggravated assault. At a follow-up trial he gave her step father fifteen hours of community service.

On her eighteenth birthday, Libby was transferred from juvie to the woman's unit at Huntsville. It took three more years for her to make parole, given some problems with other inmates.

And that's how she ended up with me. As a favor to her mother, I signed the affidavits Libby's parole officer required, confirming I employed her. Her mother—now a widow *and* twice divorced—paid me her salary so I could write Libby the paychecks she needed to prove her employment. Hiding it in my business ledger was a cinch. Libby wasn't required to actually work, and for more than a year she never crossed the threshold.

Until she did.

I still don't know why. Perhaps she was tired of closing bars every night and waking at noon. I'd like to think that, somehow, she decided to take herself seriously and learn a trade. I don't know.

All I know is that after a pleasant first week, we started to disagree. It started with display methods, graduated to the way we acquired items to sell, and was now full blown on how to manage clients and promote the business.

She saw me as old, set in my ways, and scared to make bold acquisitions or broaden my client base. When she was really angry, she attacked my hoarder's approach to keeping every record, invoice and bill related to the business.

I knew her as rash, unpredictable, quick to cut corners, and just an inch from outright breaking the law. The concept of trust, so critical to my business, was a foreign land to her. But she had a way with middle-aged men. A lean close, accidentally brush his arm with her breasts and laugh delightedly at everything he said, kind of way. With those men, each sale was just the cigarette after the act.

And then I discovered she was reaching out to my best customers, without my knowledge, inserting her clear skin, tight shiny blouses and blue-sky eyes into their imagination.

And today, the Bowie knife.

Timing, as the old saying goes, is everything.

ETIENNE BUSTO APPEARED the next day just after lunch, carrying a briefcase. As we had agreed, Libby locked the front door and joined us in my office at the back of the store. There, Busto unlocked his briefcase and placed something long and wrapped in a chamois cloth on my desk. I flipped open the ends to reveal the knife.

At first glance it matched all the requirements. The blade was longer than nine inches with a Texas clip at the point. The short hand guard was brass. The handle was bone, I guessed bison, something we could confirm later. I picked it up. It was surprisingly heavy, a good sign. The original Bowie knife had a full tang to keep the handle from breaking away from the blade, which looked like carbon steel, the right casting metal for the period. I hefted and sighted along the cutting edge, spotting a few nicks and divots. I closed my hand around the handle. It felt balanced, which, given the length of the blade, surprised me.

Holding it, I grew aware of Libby staring not at the knife, but at me. I glanced at her and she moved her hands slightly in reminder. She held a pair of kid gloves and another of latex. She was right. Normally, I would wear gloves to handle an artifact of this kind. It was something I always did to impress buyers, and add a bit of showmanship.

I ignored her. "It seems the basic requirements are in place," I said quickly to Busto. "The metal, the size, and the general form matches written descriptions. I would like an expert to examine it, if you are willing."

"Of course." Busto waved his hand, clearing the air of this tedious complication.

"Is there any family lore connected to it?" Libby asked. "Perhaps something passed down about how General Santa Anna gained possession?"

Busto smiled at her, and it was the politician's smile. "Unfortunately, no. Perhaps there was once. Our family has so many items such as this. If there was a story, it was lost many years ago."

"Thank you." Libby was uncharacteristically deadpan. I was impressed by her question. Something in my teachings had actually stuck. She understood how a story enhanced the value of any antique.

With that, I explained our appraiser was out of town and we needed a week to verify the knife's authenticity. I gave Mr. Busto a receipt and locked the knife in my safe.

As soon as the front door clunked shut Libby spun to me. "Can I look at it?" Her eyes glowed.

"Sure." I watched her skip through the store to my office.

Possibly I was mesmerized by the way her jeans clung to her.

Later, I found her sitting at my desk, wearing latex gloves, holding the blade close to her eyes in riveted concentration. Her cheeks were flushed.

"It's something, isn't it?" I smiled at her. "I mean the history of it. I thought you asked a smart question about whether there was a story connected to it. We need that."

"Uh huh." She lowered the knife and looked at me. "And you still want to sell it privately, not hold an auction?"

"It's the best way."

She stared at me for a time, before replacing the knife in the safe. Then, carefully, she removed the latex gloves, stood, and circled the desk. She stopped barely a foot from me. "Perhaps there's something we could work out. I mean an agreement." Then, in a single movement, she grasped my belt and tugged me against her. Her breasts crushed into my chest, our lips inches apart.

Heat shot through me, as did a vision of her mother splayed on the broad back seat of my father's 1968 Chevy, her cut-off blue jeans around one ankle. I tasted cherry gum. I yanked myself away. "No! What are you doing?"

She smiled at my fluster and shock, looking down at me. "Too much for you?"

"This is inappropriate," I stammered.

"Appropriate, inappropriate. Spend a few years in jail and tell me the difference."

I back pedaled out of my office. "That's not the point." I sucked in a breath. "You should leave."

She followed me into the showroom. "Think about it. We have an opportunity here, you and I." Her voice shifted from conspiratorial to husky. She leaned so close her breath tickled my ear. "Bid the knife and let's have some fun, you and I."

"Private sale," I stammered.

"Such an opportunity," she said. "Think about it. And you should know, I learned to do sooo many things with my mouth, when I was in prison." With that she collected her purse, gave me a lingering look, and left the store.

It took me an hour to calm down, and I was glad when six

o'clock arrived. I locked the shop and drove into the Stop Six area of Fort Worth, to a small bar I know. My hands felt weak. I needed a drink.

I ordered a double whiskey and a draft of Lone Star beer and carried them to the last booth in the row. I slid inside, ignoring the man across from me. I sucked down the whiskey and sipped the beer. The man looked up, a short glass of tequila cradled in his hands.

"You okay?" he asked.

"Yeah." I grinned. "You nailed it with Busto. Best character you've done. She bought it, hook, line and sinker."

Etienne Busto, or should I say, Carlos Hernandez, long-time member of the same amateur theatrical troupe as my wife, blinked slowly in satisfaction and sipped his tequila. "Told you I'd nail it."

"I liked the strut. And you did imperious so well. That bit with kissing her hand? Man."

Carlos spread his palms as if to ask, How could I get it wrong?

"And wherever you had the knife made, it was right on the money." I fished in my coat pocket for an envelope and slid it across the table to him. "As agreed."

Carlos flashed his eyes at me. "Doing my craft and getting paid for it. You gotta love America."

We clinked glasses and drank.

PERHAPS I HAVE not been completely honest with you.

But, with antiques (and given my age, I am almost one myself), I believe the value of something is in the story it tells. I tried to teach Libby that fact, and, as it turns out, she was a very good student.

I didn't see Libby after our argument. Two days later I unlocked the shop, checked the safe, and, as I expected, the knife was gone.

Of course it was. She was too rash, too careless. Too interested in the quick score, not the longevity of the business. I had expected her to steal the knife and sell it on her own. When she did, I was betting, she would be exposed as a fraud, ruined, and sent back to jail. I would be free of her. Perhaps I should simply have fired her, but she didn't actually work for me, and I didn't want her mother angry with me. Once Libby was back in jail my plan was to sympathize with her mother, commiserate with her—perhaps with a bottle or two of wine— and in time strike up our old relationship.

As a result, I wasn't surprised when, the next afternoon, two men in sport coats, white shirts and cowboy hats entered the store. They introduced themselves as Texas Rangers and asked me for identification. Their arrival was faster than I expected, but, as a rule, Libby moved quickly.

Their question about when I last contacted Judge Thomas—my long-time client who collected Texas frontier memorabilia—surprised me. I explained I talked to him every few weeks.

"Not last night?" one of them asked, leaning over the counter with a leer. He was tall and lean with a chin that could have broken icebergs.

"No," I said.

"You know," he said, "we came across your fingerprints on something in the judge's house. We know they're your fingerprints, because we have them on file. Something about a school break-in and a hog. From years ago."

"Yeah, funny story, that," I said, warming to tell it.

He cut me off and asked my whereabouts from the night before. I recounted how I went home alone and watched television.

Apparently, as alibis go, that one is useless.

The trial was blissfully quick. The story spun to the jury by the Fort Worth assistant district attorney was that I visited the good judge one evening after work, just after his wife went out with friends. We argued over the authenticity of the Bowie knife and, in my rage, I stabbed him to death. My fingerprints were on the handle. A shirt hidden in the bottom drawer of one of my filing cabinets was saturated with the judge's blood. The search history on my office computer revealed a request for directions to the judge's house, two hours before his death.

But Libby was his star witness.

Dressed demurely and speaking in a halting, pained voice, she explained how, once she began working for me, I became increasingly possessive of her. How I forced her to provide me with sexual favors under threat of telling her parole officer she was skipping work. And that, as time went on, how my outrage with Judge Thomas—and the way he treated her unfairly by sentencing her to juvie and jail—spiraled into obsession. And that, finally, as revenge, I hatched a plan to sell the judge a counterfeit Bowie knife and use the money to steal Libby away from Texas.

No one seemed to mind that Etienne Busto was nowhere to be found. Or where the knife came from. The jury just smirked when I explained the knife was a ruse.

Libby really could tell a story.

Death row in Huntsville has an oddly detached feeling. For a time, I worked through appeals, but the legal system wasn't interested. After all, I am guilty of murdering a judge. My only visitors were lawyers, until my savings were exhausted. In my last meeting with them I signed bankruptcy papers.

Several months passed before a guard announced a visitor. When I sat down in front of the small window, Libby was waiting on the other side, holding the telephone handset to her ear. I suppose I could have refused the meeting, but I was interested.

She was unchanged from the last time I saw her. Her eyes were the Kansas-sky blue I remembered, her blouse unbuttoned all the way to Mexico.

I picked up my own handset with a jaunty air. "How about that Bowie knife?"

She rolled her eyes. A moment later, "You know what tipped me off?"

I waited.

"You didn't wear gloves the first time you looked at it. You always wear gloves. Especially for something like that."

"Maybe I was too excited."

"And nicks on the blade that are clearly machine tooled? A week to authenticate? Are you kidding?"

I didn't know what to say.

"I want you to know." She looked over my shoulder and for a moment I thought I saw disgust in her eyes, unless I confused it with anger. "A few months before the knife showed up, I went through your files. All of those invoices and records from all the years. You know what I found?"

I shrugged. I didn't understand.

"Invoices from my father. You owed him almost one hundred thousand dollars when he died. You never repaid my mother."

"I guess I forgot." It came out as a croak.

She waved a hand. "I don't believe that for a second. But it's okay. When you filed for bankruptcy, I went to the hearing. Showed the invoices to the judge. Turned out, my mother and I were your largest creditor. So, I asked for your shop and the inventory. The judge gave it to me."

There was nothing to say and I stayed quiet.

She smiled, the sneer-smile rich people use when tossing coins to the homeless. "I just wanted you to know."

I sat up. "And I want you to know that I'm glad you stabbed the judge. He told me what happened to you. He victimized you. He had it coming."

She stayed silent. She knew our conversation might be recorded. Finally, slowly, she whispered, "Just so you know, I'm going to find the real Bowie knife. Sell it my way." Her eyes glittered.

I was impressed. She really had learned well. She was already to the point of believing her own stories. But she still hadn't learned that you always need a good punch line.

That's why, when it comes to stories, I'm still the master.

My punch line is a needle of pentobarbital.

**Peter W.J. Hayes'** short mystery and crime fiction has appeared in a variety of publications, including *Black Cat Mystery Magazine*, *Mystery Weekly*, *Best New England Crime Stories*, *The Literary Hatchet* and two Malice Domestic mystery anthologies. One story, "The Black Hand," was selected by the blog Little Big Crimes for the feature "The Best Mystery Story I've Read This Week." I'm also the author of two Vic Lenoski police procedural novels, with a third scheduled for publication in September 2020..

# SWITCHBLADE

100 PROOF
MODERN NOIR

OUTLAW
SINCE 2017
TALES
WITHOUT LIMITS
POLITICALLY INCORRECT

## SWITCHBLADE

QUICK & DIRTY
SHARP & DEADLY
ANTHOLOGY
OF NOIR
LOS ANGELES

THE WORLD'S **ONLY** NO-LIMIT
NOIR DIGEST MAGAZINE

ACCEPT NO SUSTITUTES
www.switchblademag.com

*The engine of survival cannot be pre-programmed.*

# These Violent Delights

## Mandi Jourdan

ISIS SQUEEZED HER pistol's warm trigger and her shot hit the man five yards in front of her between the eyes. The plasma bolt seared into his skin, into the bone beyond it. His eyes remained open even as he crumpled to the ground beside ten others that Isis and the others had killed. All around her, the spray of gunfire cut through the night, screams ending half-finished, the smell of burned flesh thick in the air. She lowered her gun and approached the man slowly.

She and the other androids had arrived half an hour earlier, and within the first few moments, they had destroyed half of their enemies' front line. Then they had made quick work of the rest, apart from the one who had escaped into Dahab.

*Programmed to kill.* Isis had read the words in her file that morning, while Hathor and Bastet had distracted the guards. The androids' files were off-limits, but they needed to know what exactly had prompted the Division to create them. Isis hadn't been sure what she'd expected to find. She'd been built with superhuman strength and trained to fire every weapon from a handgun to a grenade launcher, and still, she'd hoped there was more to what her creators wanted from her than forced military service.

Still, the words had freed something within her. Now that she knew she wasn't destined to blend into human society someday, to have a life of her own, she supposed it didn't matter how far she took the deadly gifts she'd been given. Tonight was her first real mission—the first one for all seven

androids the Division had designed. They'd been sent after a terrorist group. An enemy of their creators' country.

When one of their targets had escaped, Ra had been the one to decide that the androids should follow. He'd given the order to destroy the whole town. *We'll send a message,* he'd said. *No one will dare attack our people again, once they see what we can do.*

As Isis reached the man she'd just shot, she crouched at his side, studying him. He wore a civilian's clothes, and at this distance, the fear in his still-open eyes was easier to see. Officially, the androids were only here to take out the terrorists. But Ra's reasoning had made sense to her. Even if these civilians had done nothing wrong, their deaths would send a message to the people who had.

Footsteps approached on the sand and paused at her side. "Nice shot."

She looked up to find Osiris standing beside her. His white-blond hair was several shades lighter than hers, and he had olive skin and the same emerald eyes as the rest of the androids, though his smirk was all his own. It seemed to tell her they shared a secret the rest of the world didn't know and wouldn't condone, and a smile played on her lips at the sight of it. A heartbeat later, she forced the expression away. She reminded herself that the fluttering in her stomach at the sight of him was a trick. Their creators had programmed her to feel it—named them after a pair of married gods and decided their future before they had drawn breath.

Still, when he holstered his pistol and offered her a hand, she took it and let him pull her to her feet. "Thanks," she said. She scanned the area. Palm trees and tourist shops were aflame, out of reach of the Red Sea beyond the beach. Bodies littered the ground. Isis had lost track of how many people she'd killed, and her targets blended with those of the others, people still sitting in cars that were either bent beyond repair or burned beyond recognition.

Hot air whipped Isis's face as Ra moved at his top speed to stand on her other side. Minutes earlier, she had seen him outrun a group of cars trying to leave the town. He'd thrown one of them into another and pulled the survivors from the wreckage to deal with them one at a time.

"I think we're done here," Ra said.

As the rumble of approaching vehicles hit Isis's ears, she froze, listening hard. These engines were larger than those of the civilians' cars—V8 by the sound of them. They were too familiar.

"The Division," she said, glancing from Ra to Osiris, whose lips were pressed into a tight line. The three of them turned toward the sound as the other androids fell in on either side of them. As one, Isis, Osiris, Ra, Hathor, Horus, Anubis, and Bastet faced the small group of black Division SUVs that raced toward them. When the vehicles stopped, soldiers poured out, their weapons trained on the androids.

Isis's stomach lurched. She exchanged another look with Osiris, whose pale brows were drawn as he scowled. One of the black-clad soldiers held up a small radio, and from it poured the commanding alto of Clarisse Mitchell, the Division's leader.

"Stand down."

*Our mother,* thought Isis bitterly. Clarisse had overseen the androids' creation—from what Isis had gathered from the files she'd snuck into, President Hartley had designated her to do so—but she had never shown any of them the slightest affection. She'd studied them and tested them and ordered her soldiers to fire at them to make sure they could stand it, but she'd never cared about any part of them other than what they could do for her.

The androids didn't move.

"Why?" asked Ra. He stared at the soldiers, who still pointed machine guns at the line standing in front of them. Ra held his handgun, his fingers flexing around its grip. "Didn't we do our job?"

"Stand down now," Clarisse commanded. "You're coming back to base."

*For a moment, no one moved. Isis studied the faces of the soldiers, and though most of them were stoic, she spotted fear in the eyes of some. She raised a brow. Did we do something wrong? Aren't they supposed to be proud?*

Osiris took a step forward, and Isis heard one of the other androids let out a breath. In her periphery, she saw Ra holster his weapon, and one of the soldiers lowered his by an inch. Osiris walked toward them, and Isis followed, the smell of burned flesh still flooding her senses.

ISIS FOUGHT TO ignore the pounding of her mechanical heart in her throat. She sat at the low metal table in her assigned room at West Point—blank gray walls, white sheets, a telesense she never turned on—and listened to the hallway beyond her door. Footsteps passed her room every now and then, voices whispering things she already knew. She and the others were in more trouble than she'd realized back in Dahab. The United States government didn't just want to distance itself from what the androids had done, it wanted to distance itself from them altogether. Wash its hands of them.

*Isis ran her fingers over the notches she'd made in the underside of the table. She didn't need to count them to know there were ninety-three. One for each day since she'd first opened her eyes in a Division lab and had been given a name and a mission. Her official name was "03"; only Ra and Osiris had been created before her, and anytime one of the others—usually Hathor—tried to give her orders or disobeyed one she'd given in their combat training sessions, she reminded them of that. But Clarisse had wanted something more personal to call each of them. Something powerful. Isis's lips twitched. Sending us to fight in the country whose gods' names you stole? That's cold, Mother.*

"They're too dangerous," said a low male voice in the hallway. "If they can't be controlled, Hartley wants them shut down."

Isis's fingertip paused on the notch she'd carved that morning with the tines of her fork. She'd wondered why the Division's scientists had built her with the need to eat, and she'd come to the conclusion that they hadn't wanted her to be completely self-sustaining. They'd wanted her to need them.

"I can control them," insisted a second voice. Isis recognized this one instantly—Clarisse. "They made one mistake. That doesn't mean we can't still fix this."

"It's too late. She's made it an order. She's on the phone in your office."

Clarisse sighed, and two sets of footsteps retreated and disappeared.

Isis pushed back her chair, its metal legs screeching against the white tile floor as she stood. She paced the length of her room in six steps, turned on her heel, and started back toward the door. If she sat here and waited for Clarisse to choose loyalty to her and the others over loyalty to President Hartley, she knew she would be disappointed. And, soon after, dead.

She pressed her ear to the cold metal of her door and listened. Apart from the soft whir of the ceiling fans outside, the hallway was quiet. Isis reached for the doorknob. She swallowed and turned it, twisting hard when the lock resisted. The metal creaked and snapped, and in one swift motion, she pulled the door open by its broken knob.

All at once, the air was filled with the wail of sirens.

Isis ran into the hall, scanning the area frantically. The other androids' rooms fanned out on either side of her. If the alarms were already sounding, she saw no need for subtlety.

"We need to get out of here," she called to the others through their doors. "You know they're going to shut us down. Don't give them the chance."

One by one, the androids burst from their rooms. As Isis heard the Division agents running toward them, she looked to Osiris, who was watching her with pride in his eyes.

WHEN SHE ARRIVED with Osiris at the abandoned diner, Hathor and Horus had already settled into a long booth with cracking red upholstery. Horus sat by the window, Hathor leaning back against him with her feet resting in the booth beside her. Her scarlet hair blended with the leather. The lights were out, but the streetlamps cast enough across the tile floor for Isis to see.

She glanced out the glass front doors, and when she saw nothing in the glow of the lamps apart from a few cars parked outside nearby buildings, she told herself to relax. Since the seven androids had escaped from West Point, they had met here at least once a month to check in with one another. It was always stiflingly hot here—even now that September had begun, summer still refused to loosen its hold on the city, and the heat reminded Isis of the beach in Dahab. Of the bodies scattered on the sand, baking in the sun.

The only one she saw outside of these meetings was Osiris. The night they had all run away, dodging bullets and taking hits they'd tended to for one another afterward, Isis had known they had chosen correctly. The Division agents had shot at them the moment they'd disobeyed, and any guilt she would have felt about killing a few of the agents on the way out had instantly deserted her. They were no more her people than those she'd killed in Dahab.

That night, they had run as quickly as their legs would carry them, only pausing a few times to see whether they were being followed, and they had made it to Staten Island in just under two hours. Osiris had found the diner and pried off the boards covering its doors so they could enter, and after they had all agreed that splitting up and lying low was the best option, he'd stayed behind with Isis. He'd praised her for getting them all out of West Point, and they'd had sex on the bar.

"Where are the others?" Osiris asked Hathor and Horus.

Hathor sat up straight, drumming her scarlet fingernails against the plastic surface of the table. She wore a tight black dress and high heels. *She's enjoying this "blending in" thing,* Isis thought, resisting the urge to roll her eyes. *So eager to look like a human.*

"I assumed they were behind you," said Hathor.

"They're late," said Osiris. Isis followed him to the booth, and he slid in across from the other pair. The upholstery squeaked beneath her as she sat next to him. He laid a hand on her knee just under the hem of her pencil skirt, and her skin burned at the touch.

"It's less suspicious if we don't all come in at the same moment anyway," said Horus. He ran a hand through his copper hair and glanced out the window, and Isis followed his gaze. Down the street, she saw a human couple walking a large spotted dog. *Could I take care of a pet? Would it love me, or would it be as scared of me as those agents were?*

"Any news?" Osiris asked the others.

Hathor shook her head. She opened her mouth, but before she could speak, a rusty tinkling and a rush of air told Isis the front door had opened. She turned in her seat to watch Anubis and Bastet enter. They looked like any other couple she might have passed on the sidewalk—dark skin, short-sleeved shirts, jeans, designer shoes. Only their emerald eyes gave them away as inhuman.

*Why do all of them look like they're having an easier time playing the part than I am?* Isis had bought a wide enough variety of clothes to blend in with any crowd, but she never felt at ease when she was surrounded by humans no matter where she was.

Anubis paused long enough to watch the door swing shut behind him, and then he followed Bastet toward the booth where the others sat. He folded his arms across his chest and remained standing while she settled at the edge of the bench beside Isis.

"We have a problem," said Anubis.

Isis frowned. Below the table, Bastet's hands were shaking.

"What is it?" Osiris's voice had taken on a sharp edge, and his grip on Isis's knee tightened.

"Ra's dead."

At Anubis's words, everyone froze.

"What?" Isis blurted at last, frowning as she looked from him to Bastet and back again.

"We were supposed to meet him this afternoon, but he never showed," said Bastet.

"That doesn't mean–"

"It means," Bastet pressed on, ignoring Hathor's interruption, "that whoever they sent after him did a better job than the guy they sent after me."

"What are you talking about?" Isis asked as she shifted in her seat to face Bastet. Osiris maintained his grip on her knee. "They sent someone after you?"

"Not just me. Each of us." Bastet sighed. "I got that much out of my assassin before I slit his throat. The Division doesn't want to let us go."

"We went to the apartment Ra's been using," said Anubis. "Everything he owned was gone. They got to him."

Nausea swept over Isis. She laid her hand on the one Osiris kept on her leg.

"Or he ditched us," said Hathor flatly.

"He wouldn't," Bastet snapped. "He was working on a plan to take them down. To make us all safer."

Hathor shrugged, clenched her jaw, and turned away, staring at the bar.

"While Ra's death is a terrible loss," Osiris began slowly, "we will survive. Go home. All of you. Or leave the city—if we spread out, they'll have a harder time tracking us. Send me word when you've taken care of your assassins, and then we'll decide what to do about the Division."

For a moment, the group was still. Isis felt her pulse in her throat. As the first of the seven to be created, Ra had been their de facto leader. Osiris had been born second, but she had no idea how willing the others would be to answer to him.

Bastet slid from the booth and started from the door. Anubis followed her, wrapping an arm around her waist. Hathor sighed as she stood, and she took Horus's hand, pulling him up after her. After the four of them had filtered out and the front door had closed behind them, Isis turned to Osiris. He inhaled.

"You trust me, don't you?" he asked. "To lead us?"

"Of course," she said.

"I won't let anyone hurt you." He was watching her, but his bright green eyes were distant, as though his thoughts lay elsewhere. The hint of a smirk played on his lips, and she remembered the way he'd looked at her in Dahab, when he'd complimented her shot. For the first time, she wondered whether he'd really been proud of her or whether he'd been proud of himself for realizing she'd wanted his approval.

"I know," she said. She hoped he couldn't somehow sense the knot forming in her stomach.

THE HIGH-PITCHED ringing of her disposable cell phone

woke her, and she sat up quickly, determined to silence it before it could wake Osiris too. He lay on his back, the navy sheets draped over him lazily, one arm hanging over the edge of the bed. He didn't stir. Behind him, outside the glass balcony doors, the city was dark.

Isis grabbed the thin silver phone from the nightstand. Instead of a name she recognized, the projection above the screen read "Blocked Number." She frowned and rejected the call, but before she could lie back down, the ringing cut through the air again. She looked to Osiris. His face was still peaceful and blank.

With a sigh, she climbed out of bed and slipped into the living room, holding the phone to her chest to quiet its shrill sound. She settled onto one end of the plush white sofa. The apartment had been paid for with money Isis had stolen from a string of banks in Queens, and Osiris had told her to spare no expense with the furniture. *The humans owe us this much*, he'd said.

She answered the call and pressed the phone tight to her ear. "What?"

"Isis."

Her mouth went dry at the sound of Clarisse's voice.

"Don't hang up. Please."

Isis laughed. "Give me one reason."

"I can protect you."

"From what? *Your* people? The only danger to us is you."

Clarisse sighed. "Someone is coming for Osiris."

Silence fell like a thick curtain over the living room. Isis felt her rapid heartbeat vibrating through her chest.

"They're on the way now," said Clarisse after a moment. "And I know how you feel about him, but–"

"You should," Isis said flatly. "You've seen every synapse of my brain, haven't you?" She wanted so badly to believe there was a rational explanation for the way she felt about Osiris. She'd seen the glint of pride that hadn't left his eyes all night after the others had obeyed his commands without a word, and when he'd undressed her, she'd told herself the way he'd looked at her was love. He'd saved her life during the escape from West Point—deflected a plasma bolt that would have hit her in the temple. He'd put himself between her and the soldiers multiple times. He'd taken shots meant for her. On the way to Staten Island, he'd held her hand for seventy miles.

He loved control. But he loved her, too. She knew it.

"Isis, if you leave now—if you come home—I'll call off the person who's coming after you personally. If you let us deal with Osiris, you can walk out of there, and you have my word that no one will harm you."

Her palms tingled, and she flexed her fingers, glancing toward the locked front door. "Why would I trust anything you say?" she asked quietly.

"I wouldn't be calling you if I weren't serious," said Clarisse. "Why would I warn you unless I legitimately wanted to give you a chance to save yourself?"

Isis looked to the cracked bedroom door. She felt Osiris's hands against her cheeks, in her hair, his lips caressing hers. That night, when they'd come home from the diner, he'd told her he would rule this world and she would share it with him. He'd given her that smirk that told her they shared a secret no one else could ever know, and she'd believed him.

"I can take care of myself, Mother," she said into the phone. "You made sure of that. I don't need your permission to survive."

She ended the call and dropped the phone onto the sofa, pushing herself to her feet. She moved toward the bedroom, and before she reached the door, it opened. Osiris stood on the threshold, watching her with a raised brow. She wondered whether he'd ever been asleep at all.

"It was Clarisse," she said. "Someone's coming for you."

The sound of glass shattering filled the apartment from behind Osiris. He turned toward the noise, and Isis followed his gaze to see a black-clothed man slipping through the destroyed balcony door. The man raised a pistol, taking aim at Osiris's head, and Isis hurtled toward the intruder as quickly as she could move. Before the man could fire, her fingers were around his throat and his hand. She snapped his wrist, and the crack of his bones echoed in her ears along with her pulse.

The gun fell from his hand as he screamed. She squeezed his throat, and his scream dissolved into coughs and gasps for air. She didn't release him until these sounds had stopped along with his breath. She dropped the man to the floor with a thud.

Osiris's footsteps approached her, and when she felt his hand at her waist, he spoke to her softly. "I love you."

A smile crept onto her lips. "I love you, too," she said.

**Mandi Jourdan** graduated from SIUC with a BA in English/Creative Writing and a minor in Classics. She is the author of *Lacrimosa*, *Veritas*, and the *Shadows of the Mind* collection, among numerous other publications. She won the Missouri Review's Miller Audio Prize for Prose in 2019 with her short fiction piece "Inheritance." *The Shadows of the Mind* podcast based on her novel series is available on all major audio platforms. When not writing and listening to eighties rock, she spends time with her cats. She can be found on Twitter (@MandiJourdan) and Instagram (@mandi.jourdan).

"I come in peace."

*When spending spiritual currency, invest wisely.*

# Ghost Town

## "Doc" Clancy

THE REV. HOLYOAK had found himself in Arizona again, chasing down another lost soul. Christine Whitt's daddy was convinced that it was more than her just running away. He was sure it had something to do with a local legend about

a string of ghost towns full of dead men. Actually, Holyoak would have used the word obsessed. He wasn't sure how Whitt had found him, or where he'd connected his daughter to the gruesome legend, but he didn't ask those kind of questions. He went where the Lord led him.

So far, none of his leads had panned out, but his digging had put him into contact with the Silver Sabremen Lodge in Prescott. He had found this men's club to be mostly a bunch of meddlesome kooks, but their fascination with the obscure and occult, initially seeming to be only that typical of fraternal organizations of bored middle-class men, only disturbed him more when found to be not only genuine but exceptionally well-studied. Fortunately, they were generous with their knowledge and had been allowing him supervised access to their library.

Today his watcher was a graying, subtly widening Greg
Hilsson. Holyoak had been given to understand that Hilsson
was something of an important figure in the Sabremen,
himself visiting from back East. Looking at him in his plain
suit and rhinestone decorated fez, he sensed that he certainly
felt himself to be important and couldn't help but wonder why
he'd volunteered to watch him.

"I think you'll find this volume has a more precise telling of
the legend," Hilsson said, placing a heavy volume on the desk
next to him. Holyoak nodded curtly and kept reading. Hilsson
sat back down and watched him, and after a moment, Holyoak
took a look at the offered tome.

"Thank you," he said gruffly.

"You know," Hilsson said, crossing his palms in his
lap and letting his head roll to one side. "We've heard of
you, Reverend."

"And?" he asked, lifting his gaze from the page.

"Well," Hilsson continued, sucking air between his teeth.
He had a broad, midwestern way of speaking that made
Holyoak impatient. "A mysterious town, in league with the
Devil, halfway into death, raiding the world of the living…
This legend you're investigating—just why has it called
your attention?"

Holyoak let the book lie on the table. "A girl went missing.
Her father seems to think this 'legend' has something to do
with it."

"And what, Reverend, do you think?"

"I've seen enough in my days—especially in this desert."

"We know." Hilsson sat back, satisfied.

"Where did you lot find this book?" Holyoak asked. He had
expected another conflicting, vague account, but this book
had an entire chapter about a cluster of failed towns about
a hundred miles west that had been believed wiped out by
plague in the 1850s but from which mysterious raids appeared
to originate for decades after. It went on to detail how
someone named "Brother Tull" had wiped them out, finding
them corrupted by supernatural evil.

"There are maybe a couple of dozen copies of that book

in the world. It's not a book you'll find outside of one of our
Lodges. The Tull that this book speaks of was the founder
of this Lodge that you're sitting in now—one of our heroes,
especially for our brothers in Arizona."

"But if this Tull wiped them all out—"

"Tull himself suspected that there was one town that he
couldn't find: a place called Delilah. But he never picked up
that there was a pattern." Hilsson pulled a piece of tracing
paper from his pocket and pulled the book towards him.
Holyoak craned his neck to see him place it over the map in
the book. Drawn on the translucent paper was a complicated
sigil. "This is the sign of Pestilentia," he said. Laid over the
map its points lined up exactly with the locations of the extinct
towns. "And this," Hilsson said, pointing to a place which was
empty on the map but indicated by a long limb of the bizarre
symbol, "this is Delilah."

"Do you think it's really still there?" Holyoak asked,
knowing the answer.

Hilsson nodded slowly. "We do. We were aware of the Whitt
girl going missing, and she hasn't been the only one. We're
going to investigate now that we have some idea where to
look. In fact, it's fallen to me to decide if you should join us."

"I drive."

Hilsson pretended to be taken aback. "I didn't say you were."

Holyoak smiled, fastening the top buttons of his shirt and
replacing his white collar. "Yes, you did."

HOLYOAK APPROACHED THE town again slowly. It was
rough and unused roads took them there—roads that weren't
on any map and barely qualified as roads. It had taken hours
to navigate the treacherous country. His throat was dry and
he felt a great sympathy for the black paint job of his Bel Air,
covered in dust. He closed his eyes and whispered in God's
ear for a moment as the sparse main street of Delilah rose into
view, like something lost in time.

"What was that?" Hilsson asked from the passenger seat.
There were two of his fezzed lodge brothers in the back seat,
and they pushed themselves forward to look at the weathered

old town.

"Just a prayer," Holyoak said, his jaw clenching as he stopped the car. There were townsfolk milling around slowly.

"Good. George, did you prepare the wards?"

"Finishing them now," one of the men in the back seat said, and Holyoak heard him whispering something, chantlike and low.

"Is that a prayer?" Holyoak asked.

"No," Hilsson replied, with something like patience.

The four men exited the car and moved down the center of the street. Being closer to the townspeople, they saw that they did appear diseased. Their skin was shriveled and gray, and they moved as if insensible of their surroundings. Their clothes were old fashioned, and the colors had faded to dingy grays. A woman and her child, a little girl, almost walked into Holyoak crossing the street.

"Beggin' your pardon, sir," the woman said, averting her eyes, and he saw that much of one side of her face, hidden though it was by her bonnet, appeared to have rotted away.

A man in preacher's black stood in the street, his milky eyes unseeing as they approached.

"Welcome, strangers," he said. His preacher's collar was red and curious hooking designs were embroidered into the lapels of his coat in the same color. "Have you come to worship the Lord?"

"We each worship in our way," Hilsson responded.

"The services begin soon," the preacher said. "Come join our sabbath meal. Worship the Lord who sustains us and gives us life and strength."

The strange figure looked as if he had little of either, so Holyoak asked. "And which Lord is that?"

"Why," the old man seemed puzzled, "the True Lord, and him only."

"Of course, brother," Hilsson said, before Holyoak could respond. "We go to him now." The frail figure turned and they followed him towards the church at the other end of town. Pale figures with cold eyes observed them as they moved closer, and Holyoak, his senses alert, noticed a thin man in a

black hat who seemed to pay them special attention, stopping
to watch them as they passed.

The church itself was much like you'd find in any small
town that was old enough. The whole town in fact looked like
something out of a western movie set that had been allowed to
sit and rot. The church was the best kept building in the town,
but the top of its steeple had broken off and lay, its cross bent,
in the dirt. The paint on the church was horribly chipped and
dusty but had clearly been a deep black.

They entered the church and found it modestly decorated,
but it was a black cloth with an inverted red star stitched in
that draped the pulpit.

There was a muffled cry as two haggard beings dragged in a
girl who was roughly tied and gagged. They were dressed in
the same outdated style as the rest of the people he had seen,
and their skin seemed especially gray with their claw-like
hands against the rosy, living flesh of the girl.

In an instant, Holyoak lashed out, both of his great fists
swinging, and a brittle breaking sounded when he made
contact with the skulls of the girl's captors. Hilsson grabbed
her and quickly drew her into a circle formed by him and the
other Sabremen, whose hands shot up in an arcane gesture as
the almost skeletal figures tried to right themselves. "Christine
Whitt?" he asked, and the girl shrieked through the dirty cloth
in her mouth in response. Holyoak swung aside his thick
bomber jacket, quickly leveling a sawed-off shotgun at his hip
and blasting them apart.

A long whistle sounded from the door.

"Reeves!" the old preacher shouted, staring blindly in the
direction of the sound. Holyoak and his party turned and saw
a particularly ugly example of the type they'd been seeing in
this town. "These unbelievers have taken the sacrifice."

"Our Lord ain't gonna like that," said Reeves, letting his
words sit in the air. He pushed back the brim of his black
hat and stared at Holyoak with cold, gray eyes. His face was
so mottled and pale that Holyoak was at last certain that
the people of this town were not alive in any godly sense. A
scruffy beard framed his face and filled the deep hollows of

his cheeks, and a chip of bone protruded from the flattened hole where his nose should have been. "Nope. Our Lord ain't gonna like that a bit. Good thing Jarvis spotted them tramping through town."

He walked up to Holyoak and pointed at his collar. "You're a preacher man. You understand that sacrifices got to be made for religion. The Lord keeps us livin', but somebody else has got to pay him back."

"Tell me about your lord." Holyoak was unmoving. Reeves was dry as a husk, but there was a charnel stench on his breath.

"I told you!" the preacher interrupted. He seemed baffled by their ignorance. "We serve and worship the True Lord of the Earth and under-the-Earth. The Lord Satan."

"Now we're getting somewhere." Holyoak said, leveling his shotgun at Reeves.

"Oh, holy man," he mocked. "Where was your God when this town was poor and hungry and dying from the sickness? Where was the Lord of Heaven when the babies sucked at their mama's cold titties and the hounds picked at the bones of their masters? So our new god likes a little nip of blood now and then, and likes to watch us raise a little hell. We've been here all these years, and we ain't going on account of you."

"It was when the pox came that we called him," the preacher interjected. "Oh, we called him and he came. He cleansed the valley with fire and kept us all here, undying, forever. Praise him! All hail!"

"All hail," Reeves responded by rote.

Holyoak was full of righteous anger and moved the shortened barrel closer to his foe. Reeves raised his hands, but exposed a brown, toothy smile, pointing with his chin at the bodies of his men lying on the floor. At first Holyoak thought that he was seeing bugs crawl towards the corpses. It was Hilsson who shouted: "The bodies, they're reforming! Take the girl, now!" he commanded his men, and they bolted for the door with her between them. Reeves began a laugh that sounded human at first until a deep, rasping rattle entered in from somewhere in his guts.

The door of the church burst open and more of Reeves'

men entered, guns drawn. In an instant, the Sabremen were down and the girl was running back into the church. Holyoak grabbed her and rolled back into the pews, the shotgun spewing the hot lead death of the second charge. Hilsson, with a speed that surprised him, dove behind the pulpit and the hoary preacher collapsed, riddled with holes, as Reeves and his men launched an indiscriminate spray of bullets in his direction.

Holyoak shouted over the din as he reloaded, "Your father sent me. I'll get you out of this"—a bullet struck the pew by his ear—"I'm not sure how, but God will show us." Holyoak heard Hilsson's voice rising from behind the pulpit. Suddenly he stood up, shouting a word or a phrase in some dead language. Holyoak again felt a bullet fly past his head, but realized it was the same one, shooting back out of the wood. Reeves and his men fell in a pile by the door and Holyoak realized in the sudden silence that all their bullets had been turned back on them.

"How did you do that?" he asked as they emerged from their cover.

"It doesn't matter," Hilsson said. "It won't last. The spells keeping them alive are too strong. We have to go."

The girl cried out when Holyoak pulled out his bowie knife, but calmed when he cut her ropes and even smiled weakly when he removed the gag. Hilsson had already checked to find his lodge brothers dead and was heading out into the street. The girl stopped above the remains of Reeves, which sat up against the wall. She was shouting and stomping on his body, but then froze in a terror so stiff that Holyoak had to forcibly pull her away.

Hilsson was squinting in the sun as he moved towards the Bel Air, and Holyoak had to support the girl as he followed. The people of the town had come out and stood along both sides of the street, watching them with sad, dead eyes. The same woman and little girl that had almost walked into him were there and he saw the child's eyes—still innocent but so very old.

The Whitt girl remained still as they got into the Bel Air

and drove away back to the main road. They hadn't seen that Reeves had moved when she kicked him. It was only one eye that did, but it looked right at her. She felt as if he had seen her soul.

HOLYOAK SAT ALONE in the library while Hilsson held an emergency meeting with the other members of the Lodge, reflecting on everything that he had seen. Men had died and it hadn't phased him the way it once did.

Hilsson entered. "A Sabreman seeks knowledge, Reverend," he said, as if reading his thoughts. "Our brothers are resting in that knowledge now."

"Doesn't your brotherhood believe in God?" he asked.

"It is part of every Sabreman's oath that he confess to the One God—all others are false, or are his aspects."

Holyoak's eyes smoldered while he considered his words. "But that looked like some kind of witchery you used back there. Can you use the same weapons as God's enemies to do his work?"

Hilsson gestured towards Holyoak's shotgun that lay on the table like a sleeping animal. "Is a gun good or evil?"

"Man is good or evil. The gun is only an instrument."

Hilsson was silent a moment. "We are not sorcerers, Reverend. We are scientists. Keepers and practitioners of primeval knowledge. We're using that in what we believe is God's work."

Holyoak looked distant. "I know God has a mission for me. I don't yet know what it is—not the big picture of it. But he's guided my hand many times, brought me into the path of the unrighteous," he held up his hands, more the gnarled hands of a prizefighter than those of a holy man. "And through me he has struck them down." Holyoak sighed deeply. "I have prayed for him to show me what he asks of me, so that my soul can find some kind of peace."

Now it was Hilsson who considered his words. "Then we aren't so very different." Hilsson smiled. "We just don't believe in prayer."

Holyoak smiled back, indicating the shelves of esoteric

books, the trays of fine liquor, and the erotic art that lined the room. "No, this doesn't look like a church."

"I'd like to show you something." Hilsson rose, producing a large ring of keys as he led him to the back of the library. "Only those with the rank of Adept can enter this room, and only those of my rank," —he pointed to the word "Mage" emblazoned on his fez— "can admit a nonmember." There was a heavy door of iron bars there with the words LIBRIS PROHIBITIS above it. He opened it with a very old key.

There was a heavy feeling in the room. Looking around, Holyoak saw rows of ancient, leather bound books gilt with indecipherable devices and a hideous statue that seemed to move when he looked at it in the corner of his eye. The rest of the art in the room was blatantly obscene. Hilsson smiled boyishly and indicated a reinforced glass cabinet at the very back.

Holyoak drew closer as he used a separate key to open it, revealing a myriad of bottles, vials and jars, thick with dust, and a crossed pair of Colt 45s which were conspicuously shining and clean. "Is this where you keep the bat's wings and eye of newt?" he asked.

"No," Hilsson beamed. "Those reagents are not forbidden. We keep those upstairs. These" —Hilsson said, indicating the guns, "are the holy guns of Abramelin Tull, who used them to lay the walking dead in the frontier days of this state."

Holyoak felt a strange fascination for the guns. The weapons he had used up until now in his quest seemed crude. "May I?" he asked, his hands already reaching for them. Hilsson nodded and he took them up. The grips were carved with curious patterns of spirals and symbols that he had never seen before. They felt as if they had been made for his hands, but they made him uneasy.

Hilsson had a satisfied expression. "As I said, we don't believe in prayer. These are the only weapons that can break the dark magic being used to keep that town alive and in league with the darkness."

"Then why didn't we take them with us?" Holyoak asked.

"Reverend, Tull left those weapons there in that spot himself.

He made this territory safe, built this lodge, and hung those guns there. He said God was done with them and done with him and he died. No brother has been able to lift those guns from that spot for 75 years, as if they didn't want to be taken."

"That's easy to say when I've already done it," Holyoak said skeptically.

"Maybe." Hilsson looked at him gravely. "But I know all the brothers here tried when they heard about the trouble starting again. Hell, I flew all the way from Indiana to try it myself. Our mistake was pride, thinking it could only be one of us. Don't ask me to explain, but when I saw you fighting Reeves' men in Delilah I could tell: Those guns were waiting for you."

HOLYOAK COULDN'T SLEEP that night. Two men had been killed quickly in front of him. Killed by monsters of hell. This should have been his mission alone. He became aware of an icy presence and looked up to see the girl watching over him in the dark.

"What are you doing, Christine?" he asked.

"I have to go back," she said, her voice toneless except for a tinge of fear.

"You should stay with me," he said. "I won't let anything happen to you."

She hesitated, but slid into the bed beside him. He shifted, positioning himself over her and pulling her hands up to the headboard. She practically purred, pushing her hips against his and letting her eyes roll as she arched her back. Too late she found her hands tied to the bedpost. Holyoak sat up abruptly. "Sorry, Christine," he said. He stood up and moved to the door, taking the holstered guns of Abramelin Tull from the coat rack where he had hung them. "I can smell Reeves' magic on you."

Christine protested, the frosty glare of foreign influence glinting in her eyes, and she watched him as he considered placing the gun belts on his hips, only to wrap them over his shoulder.

"Too much power for you, holy man!" she spat in a voice not her own. And they did in fact pulse with an uneasy and otherworldly charge. Christine's face changed. "Help me!" she cried. "Don't let them take me back!" She shrieked and now she was pleading, confused as her own will struggled against Reeves' unnatural pull. "You must let me go, Reeves and his Lord call me!"

"But my Lord calls him to account. And their sorrows shall be multiplied that hasten after another God."

THE AIR ABOVE the dirt road that cut through Delilah wavered in the heat of the noon sun. Holyoak wiped the sweat from his brow as he squinted over the dashboard, the wheels of the Bel Air growling over the dry, soft clay. He felt for the Colt 45s that lay in their holsters on the seat beside him coiled like snakes, and drew them closer. He parked the car across from the dilapidated saloon. Reeves and his fellows stood waiting for him across the way, with black hats and with spurs on their boots, their gray-mottled skin almost blindingly pale in the harsh light. A few similarly deformed faces watched from the windows of the establishment as Holyoak opened the door and placed his own boots in the dust.

He was a broad, heavily built man, and wouldn't have looked as tall as he was if he wasn't standing by the car as he put the old but well cared for gun belts around his waist. Reeves' pale lips widened into a snarling smile as he and his men stepped forward, three on each side of him, their white, bony fingers hovering over the grips of the pistols at their sides. "You ready to try your Lord against mine?" Reeves asked, and spit a pus-filled wad of tobacco juice towards him.

"Always."

"Good," Reeves said. As if on cue, he and his men all drew. Before they got off a shot, three lay in the dirt, black blood oozing slowly from their faces. Holyoak couldn't deny that the guns felt right in his hands. Holyoak was fast, but not faster than all of them together. Two more shots rang out, missing him, but Reeves was as fast as he was and had already put two bullets into Holyoak, in his left shoulder and arm. Only now did the pain register, a thrilling shock of cold through his body coming on after the warm wetness inside his sleeve. "Blessed be the Lord my strength, who teacheth my hands to war, and my fingers to fight." He staggered forward. He could only hold onto the Colt in his left hand loosely, a mere symbol of power. But with the right he fired twice more, and two more fell, but not before one got off a shot that hit him in the right side of the chest and made him gasp for air. "My goodness, and my fortress," he continued, forcing his steps to be surer. A crack came from Reeves' gun and Holyoak felt his right leg give out. He looked down at the slick red staining his jeans and realized Reeves was playing with him. He looked up and saw him and his last remaining man watching him with a cold glee in their hard eyes. "My high tower, and my deliverer. My shield." Holyoak swayed on his feet, and Reeves' man made the mistake of aiming coyly at his head. Holyoak fired again, successfully hitting his would-be killer between the eyes before collapsing in the street.

Reeves' spurs jangled as he walked to his prone body. Holyoak looked up, the taste of bloody mud caking his mouth. "You poor bastard," Reeves conceded, leaning over him, the smell of decay and rancid black chaw heavy in his face. "You've seen the magic. My boys'll be right as rain before the sun sets, but what about you?"

Holyoak grinned, his mouth full of blood.

"What you grinnin' at, boy?"

Holyoak struggled, his voice raspy and tight. "Look closer," he managed to say, nodding his head at the gun in his right hand. Reeves face fell when he saw the signs of power carved in the grip around the name TULL. He looked at his men and saw no magic moving to restore them. He tried to back away.

"Cast forth lightning, and scatter them," Holyoak said hoarsely and shot him in the kneecap, which flew off bloodlessly in a cloud of dust. "Shoot out thine arrows, and destroy them!" Reeves stepped backwards painfully, causing the damaged limb to crack off at the knee. He fell backwards, his gun rolling away in the dirt. Holyoak dragged himself through the dusty road, past Reeves' severed shin, still standing in its boot. Reeves was whimpering softly, reaching desperately for his gun as Holyoak dragged himself up over his desiccated body.

"Satan! Help me!" Reeves screamed with a dry rattle in his throat. Holyoak thought he looked utterly pitiful, like something that you'd scrape off the bottom of your boot.

"Not as much fun when it's a fair fight, is it?" Holyoak asked. He propped himself up with his bleeding arm as best he could, and with his other hand shaking, pointed a Colt in Reeves' face. "Give my regards to your lord." The sound of the bullet split the air, accompanied by a hollow thud as the back of Reeves' head scattered, painting the dull tan of the unpaved street sticky black and gray.

HOLYOAK AWOKE SUDDENLY. The pain reminded him quickly of all the places he'd been shot, but it was the hard wood of the table at his back that had awakened him. Christine was above him, pressing down with a blood-red cloth at the wound in his chest. He could see she'd been crying but her face was concentrated and resolute—and her own. She only stared at him.

"Ah," Hilsson said, stepping into view above him. "You're awake."

"What happened?" he asked.

"Christine managed to fight off Reeves' influence long enough to tell us that you had set off here on your own. By the time we got here you'd already taken care of him and his men." Hilsson adjusted a bandage on his arm and Holyoak noticed that it had some strange script written on it. "Oh, just a little healing spell to hold you over 'til the hospital, nothing to worry about." Holyoak tried to protest but didn't have the strength and he relaxed against the rough grain of his makeshift sick bed. "That was a foolish thing to do, coming here alone."

"Maybe," Holyoak whispered, "but it was the right thing to do."

"Look!" Christine interjected. Both her hands were still pressed against his chest, but he followed her stare out the window. A crowd of townspeople was moving away slowly into the desert. He saw their preacher, his head low and shoulders slumped, walking alone, apart from the others. The little girl he'd seen before turned back and raised a hand towards him slowly before her mother took her and led her away.

"They're tired," Hilsson said sadly. "Only Reeves and his men wanted this to keep going. The rest have known for a long time that they got a bum deal and they want to rest. Thankfully, it was easy for us to release them from the spell once Reeves' magic was broken." Hilsson looked mournfully after them. "All this so that they could go on living a half a life and keep their town going in this godforsaken desert."

"They have called the people happy, that hath these things: but happy is that people whose God is the Lord."

Hilsson smiled. "I've spoken to my counterpart at the Prescott lodge and he agrees. Sacred arms like those guns choose their own partners. The brotherhood will be entrusting them with you."

"I can't–" he began, but he knew that he would.

"It's already done, and you are counted among the friends of the Lodge," Hilsson said, pushing Holyoak's tensing body back to the table. "You said God has a mission for you and we know he has a purpose for those guns. For now at least, you ride together."

**"Doc" Clancy's** work is firmly rooted in a version of America's mid-century which existed only in its own imagination, being influenced by b-movies, classic TV, and the pulps. His work has appeared in *Bachelor Pad Magazine*, *Gnarly Magazine*, *Night Owl Magazine*, *Downbeat Drag*, *Worlds of Strangeness*, and the biker fiction anthology *Smut Butt Magazine Presents Freaky Fiction* Vol 2. An Arizonan by birth, he currently lives in California's Santa Clarita Valley.

© "Doc" Clancy

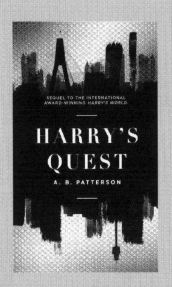

*Don't raise hell if you can't stand the heat.*

# Burnin' Love
## Timothy Friend

I LIT MY last cigarette and continued composing the epic ass-chewing I planned to deliver to Claremont when I got back. Two hours waiting in the car, nothing to do but smoke. My throat was raw and my tongue felt like an emery board. This had already turned into more work than anticipated.

The bar was a tin-roofed dive a good ways outside of Tucamcareh. If not for the cars parked in the gravel lot and the line of hookers milling outside, it would have looked like any of the other abandoned, weather-beaten buildings along the desert highway.

It was a rough place, and not where I would have expected to find Dougie Dickerson, a 40 year old firebug, short and balding with front teeth big enough to double as treadstones. I had hauled him in before and knew him to be a cowardly little shit who wouldn't give me any trouble. Plus, he couldn't have weighed more than a buck twenty if he filled his pockets with rocks.

I'd had enough hard cases with bad attitude to last me a good while, so when Claremont offered the recovery I jumped at it. Sounded like easy money until I found out from Dougie's cousin MoMo that he'd hopped in his old beater and gone to New Mexico to hook up with some woman he met online.

Even though I had the when-and-where for the hookup, I wasn't fast enough to beat a horned-up Dougie. I got there early and spotted his bright yellow rust-bucket already in the lot. Going inside and dragging him out would just invite interference from drunks and tough-guys, so I'd opted to wait.

I took my last drag and tossed the butt just as Dougie finally

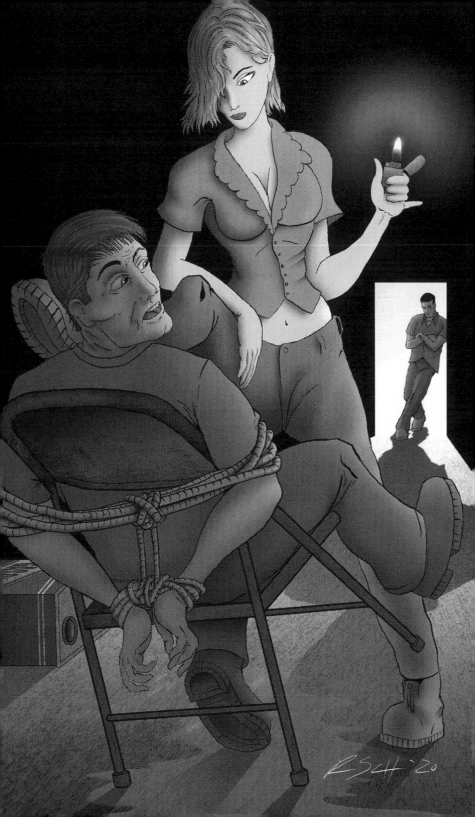

came outside. Despite what MoMo had told me it was a shock to see that Dougie actually had a woman with him, because as far as I'd known, fire was the only thing that yanked Dougie's crank. He wasn't the type of firebug that got paid for burning shit down, he was the type that got off on it.

The woman was much bigger than Dougie, not fat, but tall and broad-shouldered, wearing tight jeans and a frilly, short-sleeved blouse that showed off her muscular biceps. She had straight black hair that framed a long, dolorous face, and she had an ungainly walk, like a man.

She clung to Dougie, rubbing and pawing at him in an openly lustful manner. I tried not to let her presence aggravate me, but it did. Partly because it complicated matters, and I'd already had enough of complications. Mostly though, it aggravated me because I hadn't been laid in months and I resented Dougie. With my greying hair and pot-belly I was never going to be mistaken for a movie star, but I felt like I should be doing better than a man who resembled a gopher with alopecia.

The smart move was to follow Dougie to whatever motel he was staying at, wait for the rumpy-pumpy to finish, then barge in and slap a zip-tie on him while he was still in a post coital doze. But I wasn't feeling smart at that moment, I was feeling impatient. I hadn't driven all the way to New Mexico just to wait around while a buck-toothed firebug got his fuck on. I decided to take him right there in the parking lot.

I moved a hand to my back to make sure my .38 was in place, grabbed the stun baton and a gimme cap from the backseat, and got out of the car. I put the hat on, pulled it low, hiding my face in case Dougie happened to spot me. I walked like a drunk as I headed toward the two lovebirds, too careful, too slow, over-compensating for impairment.

As I closed on Dougie and his date, a third party joined the pair. A young man in his twenties, dressed in jeans, a plaid shirt rolled at the sleeves, and a pair of green and red two-toned bowling shoes. He was all smiles as he caught up with them. He looked like a farm boy out for a wild time, half-drunk and over the moon at the thought of scoring. I figured

that excitement would turn to regret once his buzz wore off
and he was confronted with the harsh reality of a three-way
with Dougie.

Regardless of the new arrival, I was committed to making
the grab right here and now. I held the stun baton down by
my side, patted my shirt pocket with my other hand like I
was looking for my cigarettes. The woman was closest, and
quite frankly looked like the biggest threat, so when I came
alongside the group I raised the baton and struck her on the
outside thigh. The leg buckled and she dropped to one knee
with a screech.

Dougie yelled out, "Effie."

Farm Boy jumped back, eyes wide. I pointed the baton at
him and jerked my head to the side, indicating he should
get the fuck away. He did, scurrying backwards for several
steps before he turned and ran, those ugly-ass shoes kicking
up gravel.

Dougie tried to get past me to reach Effie, but I swung
the baton around and blocked him. "Okay, Dickerson, turn
around and put your hands behind your back. Give me any
trouble and I'm going to shove this in your mouth till sparks
come out your ass."

Dougie did as he was told, but not quietly. "Fuck you,
Hogan. You're spoiling everything. You're a damn cock-
blocker is what you are."

"And proud of it." I let the baton dangle by its wrist
strap while I fished a zip-tie from my pocket and fastened
Dougie's hands.

"How did you find me anyway?"

I told him it was MoMo, because fuck MoMo.

Dougie was outraged. "My own cousin. Goddamn snitch.
Know what I oughtta do?"

"Set his house on fire and jerk off while it burns?"

Dougie gave a satisfied nod, as if to say *damn right*.

From the corner of my eye I saw Effie getting to her feet.
I was surprised she could still use that leg. The stun-baton
was a top of the line model, and I'd had a friend make a
few adjustments to crank up the juice. Cussing me from the

ground should have been the most she was capable of.

I held up one hand, palm out. "Now hold up there. I am a representative of the law and I intend to take this man back to Kansas City to stand trial for..." Shit. The paper that stated his specific charge was back in my glove box. "For burning shit down," I finished lamely.

If Effie heard me she didn't care. She grabbed my collar with one hand as she made a fist with the other. I shoved the baton hard against her left eye. There was a loud crack, like the sound of a bug zapper cranked to ten. Effie's head snapped back and she let go of me and sat down on the ground.

Dougie wailed again, "Effie. Damn it, leave her alone."

I said, "Me? Tell your woman to stop interfering in my business."

I grabbed Dougie and frog-marched him across the lot to my car. I was debating whether to put him in the backseat or the trunk when I heard the crunch of footsteps on gravel behind me. Farm Boy, I figured, coming back with something to prove.

I turned around and gestured with the baton. "Stop right there. This is all perfectly...oh, sweet Jesus."

It was Effie, charging hard and fast. Her left eye was swollen closed and twisted into a painful-looking knot, while the right one showed pure fury. Farm Boy was there too, but he stayed far back, waiting to see how things played out before he committed to rejoining the ménage.

I reached for my gun, deciding it was best to just go ahead and shoot her, but by that time she was too close. She slammed into me and I slammed into the side of my car. I lost the baton, the gun and the air in my lungs all at once. Before I could draw another breath, Effie latched onto my collar again. She started punching me in the face fast and hard. My head bounced back and forth between the car roof and Effie's fist like it was on a spring hinge. At one point I felt a broken tooth roll across my tongue, then a few more punches and I swallowed it.

As the beating wore on and on, I hoped someone would see and come to my aid. Sadly, for me, the only people who paid the altercation any mind were the hookers, and they were all on her side. I heard them shouting, "Kick his ass. Stomp him good."

And she did. She beat on my face like she was tenderizing a two-dollar steak. After a minute or two her arm must have tired, because the frequency of the punches began to slow. But just when I thought the whole thing was over she grabbed me by the throat and balls, lifted me above her head and threw me over my car. I hit the ground hard enough to knock the wind out of me again. I desperately sucked air and tried to crawl underneath the car to get away from her but she caught my legs and pulled me back, my shirt riding up, gravel scraping at my belly. She kicked me in the ribs and head more times than I can remember, mostly because I lost consciousness for a few seconds. My head cleared in time to see Dougie looking down at me, Effie beside him holding my baton.

Dougie said, "He was gonna mess up our special night."

"Mmm-mm, baby," Effie said. "Nobody's going to mess up our night."

She pressed the baton against the bridge of my nose right between my eyes, and the sun came up inside my head and exploded.

EFFIE WAS STILL beating on me when I came to. I couldn't feel it, but I could hear it. The smack of flesh striking flesh. There was a wetness to the sound and I wondered if I was bleeding and how bad.

Opening my eyes was painful, but raising my head was pure agony. The movement triggered a sharp pain in my neck along with a lot of cracking and popping. That couldn't be good.

I was seated in a chair, my arms tied behind my back with my own zip-tie. The chair was jammed into a too-small doorframe facing into a bedroom where a stained and filthy king-size mattress lay on the floor. Next to the mattress, my .38 lay beside a camping lantern that provided the only light in the room and showed me the peeling wallpaper and broken plaster that littered the floor.

Atop the mattress, Effie and Dougie were doing the do. It

was a feverish union, Dougie displaying more energy than I'd thought him capable. His pimply white ass worked like a piston, and their bodies coming together made the slapping sound I'd heard.

I felt a light breeze on my neck and looked up to see stars overhead. The chair, stuck half-in and half-out of the house, sat partially on a concrete slab of what had once been a garage, or maybe a carport. All that was left was the slab and some pieces of charred lumber and loose trash piled off to the side.

Looking to the right, I saw the first fiery glimpse of the sun overflowing the horizon and realized two things. One was that I'd been unconscious far longer than I thought. The other was that we were out in the middle of nowhere. There was nothing but barren, sandy earth and mounds of feather grass as far as I could see in the dim morning light.

As I came fully awake I noticed that my pants were soaked. For a moment I thought I'd wet myself while I was out, but then the smell hit me. Gasoline. My pants were covered in it, with more puddled around the gas can sitting beside me on the concrete slab.

Back on the mattress, Effie had a lit Zippo in her hand, fanning the flame back and forth across her nipple. She showed her teeth and hissed at the sensation. Dougie's eyes bugged out as he watched Effie toy with the flame. The speed of his pumping became frantic with pure erotic abandon.

"Easy, baby," Effie said. "Make it last a little longer, we only got the one more."

I caught a whiff of something else beneath the gas fumes. A smoky, cloying smell, like a grease trap gone uncleaned for too long. Between the smell and Effie's cryptic words I began to get a sick feeling in the pit of my stomach. In the light of the rising sun I saw that the doorframe was scorched black on the sides and overhead. That pile of charred lumber caught my eye again and I saw something there among the loose trash that I hadn't noticed before: A shoe. A single two-toned bowling shoe. Farm Boy had gotten his three-way after all, and as predicted, it hadn't been to his liking. I was just glad I'd slept through it.

I must have groaned then, or maybe it was the bones in my neck grinding together. Something drew Effie's attention and she turned her head to look at me with her one good eye. She saw I was conscious and smiled before turning her attentions back to Dougie. She clamped her thighs around his waist, dug her heels into his ass, forcing him to slow his thrusting. Next she began to move her hips to set a new rhythm, bringing Dougie along, now moving at her pace.

Despite my immediate peril, I was distracted by Effie's movements. Unlike her awkward gait, there was a hypnotic grace to the way she worked her body. Fantasizing about burning me alive must've brought out her sensual side. I gazed at the roll of her hips for a few more seconds before suddenly remembering that I was likely to die here if I didn't get my shit together. I jabbed my tongue against the remnants of the tooth shattered by Effie's beating. My head lit up with pain that burned off the remaining mental fog.

I did a rundown of my situation. My feet weren't tied, but the chair was jammed tight into the doorframe, so I wasn't going anywhere unless I got loose from my restraints. I could feel that they'd used only one zip-tie, probably because that's what they'd seen me use on Dougie. But that was because Dougie on his own posed no threat. If it had been anyone else I would have used at least two, or more likely handcuffs.

I began to twist my right wrist back and forth, pulling and working to get my hand free of the zip-tie. The stiff plastic scraped and chafed, but I kept at it. I had to keep my motions small so as not to give myself away to Effie. She kept looking over at me like a beggar at a butcher's window and I knew she was imagining me on fire and screaming. The way she kept working that lighter I figured her nipple was half roasted by now.

The skin around my wrists and on my palms was raw and painful. I was making progress though, I just had to get loose before Dougie got his rocks off. Not a race I wanted to be in, especially since his manic thrusting seemed to indicate he was already back in the red. I had the feeling that once Dougie reached the point of no return, Effie was going to toss that lighter even if she hadn't crossed her own personal finish line. Then they would both watch me roast like a campfire weenie.

The only thing I could do to slow Dougie down was distract him, so I said, "Which one of you inconsiderate motherfuckers is going to give me a handie."

Effie stopped cooking her tit long enough to look my way. Dougie kept on humping, oblivious.

I tried again, looking to hit a nerve. "I gotta warn you, I won't settle for some half-assed tug either. I want it done right, the way Dougie's mom does it. He knows what I mean. Don't you, Dougie?"

That got his attention. Dougie stopped fucking and glanced at me with a confused expression. "What the hell are you even talking about?"

Effie reached up and took hold of his chin, turned his face toward her. "Ignore him. He's just trying to put you off your game. We're so close, and we both need this. Don't let him ruin it."

Dougie pouted. "He's just so annoying. It's hard to concentrate."

Effie said, "I know baby, but you can do it."

Effie dug her heels into his ass like she was spurring a horse. Dougie started thrusting again, but his heart wasn't in it. Effie kicked at him harder, muttering encouragement and curses in equal measure. Slowly, Dougie got up to speed.

I was close to getting free. I paused and flexed the fingers of both hands while I pondered what to do once I got loose. It didn't seem like a good idea to charge them while Effie had that lighter out. All she had to do was wave it in my general direction and I was literally toast. The most urgent thing though, was to keep Dougie from popping his cork.

I said, "You guys getting thirsty? I sure am. Why don't we get Dougie's mom to bring us some Gatorade, then we can fuck her in the—"

"My mom's dead, you prick." Dougie shouted at me.

"That's what makes her such a good fuck," I said. "Dig her up when you need her, throw her back in the hole when you're done."

Dougie groaned in frustration and climbed off of Effie,

slapping at her grasping hands. Dougie bent and grabbed a sock from the floor.

"I have to shut him up," Dougie said. He came toward me with the dirty sock held out before him.

I jerked my head from side to side, but there was no preventing him from gagging me with that wad of dirty cotton. Dougie grabbed a handful of my hair and yanked my head to the side, and when I yelled in pain he jammed the sock in my mouth.

Dougie walked back to the mattress. For just a second he blocked my view of Effie and, I hoped, her view of me. I had to move now, while his back was still to me.

I pulled my hand free with a sudden painful yank and ran at Dougie. Hobbled is a more accurate description. Something was banged up in my right knee and it wouldn't straighten all the way. Dougie heard me coming and started to turn. I grabbed him by the scruff of the neck and shoved him forward. We moved together until he hit the edge of the mattress and we toppled over onto Effie, pinning the lighter between their bodies.

Effie slipped one hand free and grasped around the floor for the gun. I spit the dirty sock in her face and when she instinctively swatted at it I snatched up the .38 and pressed the barrel against her forehead.

Dougie was squirming and yipping so much I figured that Zippo must still be pretty hot down there between them. I leaned my full weight on him and he yelped louder.

Effie stared up at me, not saying a damn word.

THEY HAD DRIVEN Dougie's car to Effie's squat and left mine back at the bar. I put Dougie in the backseat and used my last tie to fasten him to the armrest. My baton was there and I moved it to the front floorboard out of Dougie's reach, then I went back inside where Effie was.

I had a decision to make. Calling the cops was out of the question. Provided the cops arrested the right people, which was never a certainty, there was still the matter of Dougie. There was no way the cops would let me take him back with me, and I didn't intend to leave New Mexico empty handed. It seemed like somebody should come out of this mess ahead, and I felt strongly that somebody should be me.

I'd put Effie in the same chair I'd been in and had Dougie tie her hands behind her back. Effie sat naked and glaring at me, already thinking about her eventual escape and pursuit I assumed. It was certainly what I was thinking about. I pulled the single ratty blanket off of the mattress and draped it over her. She didn't thank me. I knelt in front of her.

"I figure you have all sorts of ideas for when you catch up with me," I said. "And I know what you're thinking."

Effie stared.

"You're thinking that zip-tie won't hold you for long. Am I right?"

Effie's long face might have been a blank, or I maybe I saw the faintest trace of a smile. I was in no mood for uncertainty.

I pointed the .38 and shot her in the foot. She sucked in a mouthful of air to scream but before she could let it out I shot her in the other foot.

Back in the car Dougie was frantic with worry, even after I told him I'd only shot her in the foot. "She might bleed to death."

"Don't care if she does," I said. "That's what happens to assholes who try to set me on fire."

When I got back to the bar my car was stripped. All four tires gone, and the windshield busted in. The engine was still there, but it looked like somebody had taken a sledgehammer to it. Someone had shit in the front seat, and in the back too. There was also a smeared mess of it on the dash and steering wheel that told a story of over-confidence and poor coordination. And just in case I missed the godawful smell, the word SHITMOBILE was helpfully spray-painted on the side in day-glo orange.

I decided to drive Dougie's car back to Kansas City. I also decided Claremont was going to be giving me a lot more than ten percent for this job.

Dougie's clunker had no air conditioning, so I drove with the window down, letting the desert breeze blow the stink off of me and dry my gas-soaked pants. Dougie sat quietly in the backseat, staring forlornly out the window. He sighed occasionally, but was otherwise quiet, lost in romantic reverie as the smell of ash and gasoline wafted over him.

**Timothy Friend** is a writer and filmmaker from Kansas City. He is the author of *Rocket Ryder and Little Putt Putt Go Down Swinging*. His fiction has appeared in a variety of publications including *Thuglit*, *Needle*, and *Switchblade*. You can find out more about his work at <www.timothyfriend.net>.

"What do you mean you'd like a beer?
You just drank one tomorrow."

*Consequences are never considered
by the single-minded.*

# Necessary Evils
## Serena Jayne

JULIE HAD ALWAYS thought of her husband in terms of
a locked safe filled with riches. One that she'd spent four
frustrating years working to discover the combination to
unlock. But, in the emergency room, as the pharmacist, a big-
breasted bimbo in a polyester pantsuit, explained all the ways
Walter's new medicine could kill him, Julie's vision of him
morphed. He was merely a blood bag, and all she needed to
do was puncture the thin plastic barrier and the anticoagulants
would make sure the crimson contents emptied out. And no
silly prenuptial agreement would stand in the way of her
getting her hands on every last cent.

Julie recognized the gravelly voice of the ER doctor, who
had directed the pharmacist to the "deep vein thrombosis
situation" in their little white-curtained-corner of hell, calling
for a surgical consultation for one of the other patients.
Probably the man who argued with his mother about who
was responsible for the dismemberment of his pinky finger
after an unfortunate mishap with a circular saw. His mom had
forgotten to replenish their supply of zip lock baggies, which
resulted in the transport of the detached digit in a travel coffee
mug filled with ice. In another corner, an elderly woman
moaned like an animal that needed to be put out of its misery.

The unsavory smells of antiseptic, musky body odor,
blood, and the sharp stink of fear clung to Julie's silk dress. A
manicure, a pedicure, and a gallon of mimosas were required
to erase the hospital taint, not to mention a steam shower, a
blow out, and a hot stone massage.

The whole day needed to be filed under "necessary evils."

After reeling in Walter, big fish that he was, she'd collected enough necessary evils for a couple of curio cabinets.

Considering how her husband eye fucked the tiny bit of cleavage not covered by the pharmacist's lab coat, Julie's days of luxury were winding down. Trophy wives tended to have a short shelf life and Walter's brush with death no doubt accelerated the process. Why waste whatever time he had left with Julie when he could have a younger, firmer, prettier model. She couldn't bear the thought of ending each day with her hair reeking of fryer grease and flirting with Mother Clucker's repulsive clientele in the hopes of getting a couple of extra bucks' tip. Stupid prenup. Her mama taught her better than to give a man an all-access pass to her vagina without a guarantee of at least fifty percent of his assets.

The man was a joke. Bitching and moaning about how much it hurt to walk and that his foot was too swollen for anything but the stupid plastic shoes Julie forbade him to wear in public, which made his feet stink despite the weird ventilation holes. She'd agreed to drive him to the emergency room because she couldn't stand his cry baby whining. He almost looked happy when the ultrasound confirmed his blood clot.

"Take one fifteen-milligram tablet twice a day for three weeks and then one twenty-milligram tablet once daily thereafter." The pharmacist handed Walter two paper cups. One contained a tiny red pill, and water sloshed in the other. "Fill your prescription tonight so you can take your next dose first thing in the morning with breakfast. Always take this medicine with a meal."

"Jewel makes the best pancakes, but she always forgets that I prefer cinnamon butter to maple syrup." He made puppy dog eyes at the pharmacist, seeming to imply that the woman wouldn't make such a stupid mistake. If Walter hadn't let their chef and maid go a couple of months earlier, Julie wouldn't have to touch a kitchen utensil.

Walter needed to bite the dust sometime in that three-week window, while thirty glorious milligrams of blood thinner coursed through his body. After his criticism over her cooking, Julie was tempted to ask the missing pinky guy if she could borrow his saw.

"Pancakes sound lovely." The pharmacist tucked a stray strand of hair behind her ear. "A little red meat won't hurt either. Your ferritin and iron levels are lower than I'd like. While you're taking the anticoagulant, I suggest adding an over-the-counter iron supplement."

"Prescription drugs are so damn expensive. How long do I have to be on the blood thinner?" Walter squeezed the pharmacist's arm the same way he'd groped Julie's after they'd first met and she'd set down a steaming platter of chicken tenders on his table, as though his fingers were calipers, and he was making sure she met the trophy wife criteria for body weight.

The woman checked his chart. "In most cases, three months is sufficient, depending on what caused the clot, but I suspect that flight to Hawaii is the culprit."

Served him right that their tropical vacation caused his blood clot. Walter never wanted to go on that trip. He'd punished her by purchasing coach tickets, when Julie's ass deserved the luxury of first class. Their shoddy accommodations were miles away from the beach, and he'd insisted she make all their meals in the shitty little kitchenette which stank of burnt hair. Worst. Trip. Ever.

"Can't wait for the medicine to make the pain and swelling go away." Walter popped the tablet the pharmacist had given him into his mouth and washed it down with the water.

"The blood thinner won't destroy the clot. That's something your body should do naturally. We want to keep the clot from traveling to your lungs and turning into a pulmonary embolism. Call your primary care physician if you cough up blood, have any unusual bruising, dizziness, difficulty breathing, chest pain, or a serious fall." The pharmacist handed Walter a pamphlet. "Should you have an uncontrolled bleeding event, you need to head to the nearest ER. They may need to administer a reversal agent."

Pulmonary embolism. Uncontrolled bleeding event. All the deadly diagnosis talk was making Julie wet.

Once the discharge papers were signed, Walter placed his

clammy hand in hers and squeezed. "We'll get through this together, Jewel."

Julie unclenched her jaw and smiled wide enough to dis-play the dental implants in the back of her mouth. The titanium posts of the implants, which were covered by ceramic crowns, were the first precious metals Walter had bought her back in the days she still peddled deep fried chicken bits and beer. Those days she'd kept her smiles small and her dreams smaller.

All he needed was an injury to get the red fluid flowing, so the anticoagulants could work their magic. Once she inherited Walter's fortune, her evils would be based on her whims rather than on necessity.

ON THE EGYPTIAN cotton duvet, Julie set out the BDSM gear she'd ordered from the internet. Floggers. Whips. Paddles. Restraints. Riding crop. She'd purposely chosen the most heavy-duty and potentially pain-inducing of the site's offerings.

She'd diligently experimented with each item by whacking the suede couch until her arms ached, trying to elicit the most satisfying *thwamp*. The image of her husband's flesh pinking, capillaries bursting, bruises forming, blood pooling spurred her on.

The black leather corset she wore squeezed, the thigh-high boots pinched, and the tiny G-string itched, but adrenaline pumped through her veins.

Protecting the 1800 thread count sheets with plastic was prudent. Blood stains were a bitch to remove. Something Julie would never have considered before Walter had let the maid go. But once she inherited his money, she could buy as many expensive sheet sets as she liked. Maybe she'd burn down their midcentury modern house along with the memory of every necessary evil she'd performed there. She could start fresh with an upgraded life in a brand-spanking new luxury home or a sleek and sexy water-front property.

Walter, clad only in a saggy, dingy-white pair of boxer briefs, stood in the doorframe of the master bathroom, eyes agog. Sounds of what a squeezed rubber ducky might make gurgled from his throat. That was her husband in a nutshell, an extraneous bathtub toy she'd outgrown. A ridiculous impulse buy better left on the shelf.

"No." He scratched at the patchy gray hair on his chest. "Hard pass on the rough stuff."

Her hands shook. All the trouble she'd gone to, and there he was shutting her down. Trying to turn her into a submissive with a single word.

Her fingers itched to beat him to death with the riding crop. Such an overt murder would garner her the electric chair. She needed his death to look accidental.

"You're so damned vanilla," she spat. "You never want to try anything new."

"Come on, Jewel. Your outfit looks doggone uncomfortable. I prefer you in silk." He stroked the back of her neck and wrapped his arms around her abdomen. "Take your clothes off so we can make love and cuddle."

Her skin crawled as though a thousand worms writhed upon it. The only way she'd cuddle with him was if she could do it hard enough to accomplish internal bleeding.

She'd had such a great vision of him, cuffed and bruised with blood sloshing around his insides. While the anticoagulants did their thing, she'd planned to suck down Moscow Mules and conduct online retail therapy. Earlier that day, she'd loaded her virtual carts full at a dozen online retailers, but something was wrong with her stupid credit card. She must need to call and increase her credit limit again.

She decided to try another tactic. Doing her best strip tease, she removed her boots, stockings, and panties. The corset proved to be harder to shed in a provocative manner, but she tried her best.

"Come on, Wally." She wiggled her naked ass. "Give me just fifteen minutes. If you're not into the scene by then, we can do whatever you like."

But instead of paying attention to gym-honed nude body, Walter packed up the gear and placed her clothing into a neat pile.

"What kind of return policy does the place you got all that stuff from have? Can you get a full refund or do they only issue store credit?"

"Who knows?" Julie never returned anything. Even when her paychecks barely stretched beyond the necessities. Her cheeks grew hot thinking of the many times her mother had argued with customer service employees, trying to return worn clothing and broken appliances well past their warranties.

"Send the stuff back in the morning. Get a refund if you can. I mean it, Jewel. Return everything or I'm canceling the lease on your car."

She clenched her fists and her nails bit into the flesh of her palms. He cared more about the nickels and dimes he'd get from the refund and canceling her lease than having sex. Her naked body was losing its power over him. Maybe the bastard was already considering candidates for wife number three.

Julie needed a helping hand. Someone to do the dastardly deed while she arranged an airtight alibi. Luckily, she knew someone with the perfect shady connections who'd do anything for a buck.

JULIE HAD HOPED to never return to Mother Cluckers. Hoped to never breathe in the oil-laden air. Hoped to never encounter the people who'd known her when she was dirt-poor and desperate.

After a mini-panic attack at the sight of the neon dancing chicken sign, she crossed the point of no return and took a seat on a wrought-iron rooster-embellished stool at the bar. She raised her hand to get Sean's attention. Few customers claim-ed the other cock stools in the lull between lunch and happy hour.

The bartender gave a nod and went back to margarita making. Sean filled out the Mother Cluckers' uniform well. Her double D breasts strained the buttons of the gingham blouse, which she wore tied to bare her taut tummy. The inside pockets of her short shorts hung past the ragged hem, the whiteness accentuated by Sean's tanning-bed-brown skin. Her hair hung in honeyed waves. Under the stink of stale beer and fryer grease, her signature coconut-melon scent lingered.

Julie used to despise Sean. The sound of her tinkling laugh, her perfect, artificially whitened smile, and the college courses she managed to mention in every conversation.

At first, she couldn't believe Walter seemed to prefer her to Sean. Then she realized that he wanted his women a little broken, a little battered, a little hungry. Women who'd drop their panties for a fancy meal. Women who could be bought at a bargain rate.

But the last four years hadn't been kind to the bartender. Her exposed flesh looked like something shed by a scaly snake. Wrinkles etched a cautionary tale of too much tanning bed use on her face. If she still slung drinks at the chicken joint, her higher education wasn't worth a basket of onion rings.

Julie might not have a degree, but she still got carded occasionally, thanks to fancy skin creams, a regular Botox regimen, and her vampire-like aversion to the sun. No one with twenty-twenty vision would peg the bartender as anything under forty on a good day.

"On the house." Sean set a Bloody Mary down. "You look great. Marriage sure suits you. Where's Wally?"

"He's a bit under the weather." Julie imagined him six-feet under precisely and bit back a smile. "Still dating Luke?"

"Nah. He's back in the joint for violating his parole. It's for the best. Whenever he went on a bender, he turned into a mean motherfucker." Sean's brows drew closer together and the lines on her forehead deepened. "I've got lousy taste in men. I'd do anything to have someone as sweet on me as Wally is on you. He'd wait hours for a seat in your section. Made my heart flutter when he told me he'd nicknamed you 'Jewel' because you were his precious gem."

Julie ran her tongue over the implants in the back of her mouth. The ones Walter bought for her, so she'd smile bigger. The first taste of a life Julie had only dreamed of. One where she'd be the pampered princess instead of the order taker, the chicken basket bringer, the toilet scrubber.

But Walter reneged on his promise of a fairytale lifestyle. Julie's domain was no castle. No servants responded to her every order. Even her trip to Hawaii was no paradise. Like his credit card, he had limits. Julie had so little autonomy that she might as well be a figurine in a case that he occasionally dusted. No way was she going to wait to be swapped out for a newer, shinier knickknack.

"Do you keep in touch with any of Luke's buddies?" Her voice was as soft as the brush of a feather. "I need some help with a little problem."

"I learned to steer clear of his pals. Last time one of his friends said hello to me, Luke broke his hand hitting the guy."

Julie slumped in her seat. Returning to Mother Cluckers had been a dumb idea.

"Do you have a stalker or something?" Sean leaned close. "I can let you borrow the pepper spray I keep in my purse. Make sure to check the wind's direction before you press the trigger. Blowback is a bitch."

"Yeah, this guy from the gym won't leave me alone. Too much testosterone's shrunk his brain to the size of a chicken nugget. He's full on obsessed with me. I'm going to need something a hell of a lot more serious than pepper spray to get him to back off." Julie reached across the bar to squeeze Sean's leathery hand, so as to stop herself from embellishing the lie to the point that it became unbelievable. "I'm really scared. Please help me."

"You did cover for me with management that time when Luke had the bad hit of acid, and I had to spend most of my shift trying to convince him that he wasn't being eaten alive by maggots." Sean sighed. "Give me a minute."

Julie sipped her Bloody Mary and nibbled at the vegetable garnish. Luckily Luke never slipped and told Sean about all the times he and Julie had hooked up. Not that she was into thugs like Luke. All in all, she got more satisfaction in fucking up Sean's life than she did in fucking her boyfriend.

Julie loved the things Wally's money bought. The three-hundred-dollar pumps she wore would make her feet scream twenty minutes into a shift at Mother Cluckers, but their beauty topped the faux leather sneakers she'd worn while waiting tables. The shoes were an upgrade, and Julie would happily perform any number of necessary evils to prevent a backslide into a life that involved anything less than real leather shoes.

"Luke had me hold on to this for him. Felons can't get caught carrying weapons. Bad enough he failed his drug test." Sean dropped the paper bag she held with a thunk. "Thought you'd ask me to be in your wedding, and I didn't even score an invite. Guess I shouldn't have been surprised when you full out ghosted me."

"I was embarrassed. Walter forbade me from inviting Mother Cluckers staff. He's not the man you think he is." Her husband had made no such edict, but Julie wasn't about to admit that she didn't want any women in the wedding party who might steal the show. And she had no doubt that Sean would rock the fuchsia bridesmaid monstrosity she'd chosen. At least she would have four years earlier.

"He probably wanted to give you a fresh start. That man would drag the stars down from the sky for you. Walter's a keeper. I doubt my Luke would equate my worth to a hunk of quartz, let alone a jewel."

"Still taking those college classes?" It killed Julie to bring up Sean's favorite topic, but she couldn't stand for the bartender to keep gushing about Walter's virtues. Sean must have dipped into Luke's goodie bag of narcotics to imagine Walter as anything less than an albatross.

"Got my third Associates degree last year. Unfortunately, lots of companies won't settle for anything less than a bachelor's degree."

Julie took a long draw on her straw before rising.

"Give Wally a big hug for me," Sean said. "And bring that back after you give that stalker a good scare."

"Will do." Julie tucked the paper sack into her oversized designer shoulder bag, dropped the wrinkled ten-dollar bill she'd taken from Walter's wallet on the marred wood of the bar, and walked out of Mother Cluckers with her head held high, stopping for a second to give the neon sign the bird, her habit every time she'd completed a shift.

She'd hoped to hire some random thug to shoot Walter, while she established an iron-clad alibi at the spa, but, like always, she couldn't count on anyone but herself. Mother Cluckers might be Sean's destiny, but it sure as shit wasn't going to be Julie's.

JULIE COULD WRITE everything she knew about guns in the signature box of her platinum card. Luckily, all she needed to do was point the barrel at one of Walter's numerous fleshy bits and pull the trigger. She didn't want a kill shot. If the pharmacist was worried about him getting a bruise, a gunshot wound while on the anticoagulants would get the job done. All the better to make the incident look like an accident or a burglary gone wrong.

Clad in a scratchy nylon jogging suit, cheap boots, and a pair of rubber gloves, she waited for the clunky noise of the garage door assembly to signal Walter's return. She'd pinned her hair up and covered it with a shower cap.

She placed her favorite pumps in her line of vision to remind herself that shooting Walter and watching him bleed out was just another necessary evil. Soon she'd step back into those gorgeous shoes and the lifestyle they represented. Soon she'd be a rich widow. A cougar, who could prowl the dating jungle for a young stud to satisfy her sexually. Assuming she could resurrect her sex drive. Being married to Walter had shrunk her libido to a raisin-sized urge.

The garage door assembly did its spasmatic shake and her heart shimmied along.

She pursed her lips, holding the gun in a two-handed grip.

The backdoor opened and closed, and Walter's heavy tread sounded on the carpet.

Her hands trembled. She hadn't established a proper alibi. If she'd been smart, she'd have crunched up his pills and added them to the lunch she made him every day. Gotten the highest, explainable dose of anticoagulant in his system to give her the best chance at success.

Her plan wasn't any better than her mom's pathetic attempts

to return used merchandise. She was no better than the dumb broad with bad teeth she'd been nearly a decade earlier.

"Jewel?" Her husband's voice wavered. "Hon, we need to talk about your credit card spending."

Her spine turned to steel. She didn't want to live another day with a man who kept all his money to himself. She had to shoot him. If she divorced him, the stupid prenup would leave her destitute with few options beyond begging for her waitressing job back.

The sight of her patent leather shoes spurred her into action. "I'm upstairs," she called, her voice strong and sure.

As he ascended, the stairs went *creak creak creak*.

She held the gun outstretched, waiting.

"Jewel, honey. Are those shoes new? If they are, you need to return them."

With his attention focused on the shoebox at the top of the stairs, she studied him as though he were a sepia-tinged snapshot, some silly relic from the past. She took note of his salt and pepper hair, receding hairline, and the shit-colored age spots that turned his skin into a connect-the-dots puzzle. The faded blue button-down shirt, pleated khakis that made him appear to have a front butt, and scuffed shoes. His cheap cologne reminded her of the musky scent her grandpa favored. She couldn't muster any feelings for Walter beyond disgust.

He turned. His eyes went wide, and he swallowed. "Jewel? Honey?"

She pulled the trigger, but unlike the movies, no projectile exited the barrel to bury itself in the target. She fumbled, trying to find the safety, trying to salvage the situation, trying to do one thing right in her fucked up life.

Walter took one step. Then another. Reached out for the gun.

But Julie refused to release the weapon. Refused to give up on her plan.

They struggled. And finally, mercifully, the gun went off.

But it wasn't Walter who screamed in pain. Wasn't Walter who tripped over the shoebox and tumbled down the stairs, head pinballing off every surface. Wasn't Walter's blood soaking the carpet.

"Ohmygod. Ohmygod. Ohmygod," Walter wailed. "You're going to be all right, Jewel. You have to be."

Her vision blurred. She tried to speak but couldn't make her mouth work. Couldn't make anything work.

He stroked her sweaty forehead. "I'll never forget the first time you waited on me. When I ordered the shrimp scampi special, you wrinkled your nose and told me that only idiots ordered seafood at a chicken joint. You were as fierce and ethereal as a Valkyrie."

The day he mentioned blurred with every other day at Mother Cluckers. Only his big tips and promise to pay to fix her teeth were memorable. He didn't want a Valkyrie, whatever the hell that was. He wanted an indentured servant.

"I couldn't wait to divorce my wife so I could devote my life to making you happy. But clearly, you're not happy. I thought keeping you in the dark about the sorry state of our finances was a good idea. I should have told you about the bad investments, but I worried you'd leave me. But your accident gives us the second chance we need. While we've had our problems, we're not like other couples. We're meant to be together forever. For better, for worse, and for richer or poorer."

She tried to talk. Tried to drag herself away from the shit show that had become her life, but she was a human-sized doll. A mannequin incapable of movement without strings and a puppeteer.

"At least my healthcare coverage is great. We'll get you a wheelchair, a hospital bed, one of those portable potties, whatever you need. I'll arrange to work from home so I can care for you twenty-four hours a day. I'll always be by your side. Always proving my love for you."

A tear rolled down Julie's face.

He brushed away the moisture with the back of his hand and stood. "Gonna call for an ambulance. Be back in a flash, Jewel."

The only things that appeared to be working on her body were her pain receptors and her tear ducts. Julie wished she were a punctured blood bag, emptying faster than the paramedics could drive. But she knew better, just as she knew something was very wrong with her spine. She couldn't bear the thought of a future which revolved around Walter feeding her, dressing her, wiping her ass. Never again having a Walter-free moment. Every breath, every heartbeat, every second of her life becoming a necessary evil.

**Serena Jayne** received her MFA in Writing Popular Fiction from Seton Hill University. She's worked as a research scientist, a fish stick slinger, a chat wrangler, and a race horse narc. When she isn't trolling art museums for works that move her, she enjoys writing in multiple fiction genres. Her short fiction and poetry have appeared in *Switchblade Magazine*, *Space and Time Magazine*, the *Oddville Press*, *The Monstrous Feminine: Dark Tales of Dangerous Women*, *Neon Druid: An Anthology of Urban Celtic Fantasy*, and other publications. <serenajayne.com>

"You didn't indicate you were a robot on your dating profile."

*Redemption? Forget about it . . .*

# Intercession

## Adam S. Furman

JOHN KNOX STEPPED into the shadowed fear surrounding the playground. A presence around the plastic slides and monkey bars cooled the hot June night. The terror would heighten the natural senses of an ordinary man and intuitively send him away, but Knox continued onward.

The playground stood inside a park with interspersed sycamores and maples near Lisle, Illinois. Cicadas and other insects chirped through the night, the volume of which masked the sound of Knox rustling through the area.

The foul stench of sulfur tickled his nostrils. Knox adjusted his black bandana, securing it tightly over his crooked nose. Only his sullen eyes shown, weary from his past encounters. Horrors breathed death and they hold a certain power over humans.

The playground seemed to close in on him. Knox was hunting and combat with his prey would be in close proximity. Neither the custom shotgun nor his trusty six shooter would work for the job tonight. He calmly drew his dagger and it gleamed silver in the moonless night. Knox ran a coarse hand over the engraving on the dagger's blade. The blade expelled most demons back to the abyss with one slice.

The slightest movement among the flecks of wood chips drew Knox over to the carousel. As he moved closer, a crescendo of chattering teeth clicked through the sycamore trees, overtaking the buzzing cicadas.

"You might as well show yourself," Knox said, staring underneath a bridge from a rock wall to a lemon colored slide. "The jig is up."

A child's laughter echoed from inside the slide. Knox twirled the dagger in his hand and started towards it.

"No need to prolong the inevitable," Knox said.

The child's giggle then bounced off the trees. Knox turned to follow the noise. He became disoriented and lost his balance. Next he heard a thick batting of wings from above.

A weathered monstrosity descended from one of the trees. Knox only saw the mossy colored flesh as it folded its wings and extended its legs. The demon's feet made contact with Knox's chest and sent him on his back. With a quick flap of its wings, it remained unfazed by the drop kick and stood over him.

The demon drew its arm back, yellowed claws extended from its knotted fingers. Knox rolled away just as it slashed at him. He recovered, dagger clutched firmly in his right hand.

"Stick around and you can be my meal," the demon said. It spoke in its ancient language of clicks and growls.

Knox responded in English. "That's not much of a threat from something resorted to scaring little kids on the rope bridge."

The demon flashed its fangs and soared over to Knox. It tackled him to the ground and they grappled. The demon was strong, but Knox could hold his own. He threw a punch at the demon's face. The blow landed on its jaw and its skin plumed out the other side.

The demon dug its talons into Knox's arm. The pain shot up his neck causing him to spasm. It leaned inches from Knox's face and let out a deep growl. Knox clenched his jaw, determined to drive through the pain. He stabbed at the demon with his dagger.

The demon snatched Knox's wrist. He writhed in pain. It struggled to firmly pin Knox down. He felt the blackness rush his vision. His strength began fading and fear rose in its place.

With his last ounce of resolve, Knox shifted his weight and kicked the demon over his head. He grabbed the demon's arm as it tumbled over him. They rolled before Knox straightened out his leg and held firm. He twisted, managing to get on the demon's back.

The demon thrashed. Knox struggled to stay on it. The demon's head caught Knox in the nose, sending a warm blast down past his mouth. Knox grabbed the demon's head with his left hand and pressed all his weight upon it. It twisted, exposing its neck. With his other hand Knox brought the dagger to its throat.

"Wait!" it yelled in English. The demon froze. All Knox felt was its heavy breathing. "You're John Knox, right? I—can help you."

Knox pressed the blade harder against its neck. "I don't take help from demons."

"A deal? Let me go and I'll give you something you want," it said.

"Your words mean nothing, harpy," Knox said. "I don't make deals with evil."

"An intercession," it said.

Knox loosened his hold. "What?"

"There's stirrings of an opportunity," it said. "You can exchange one soul to save one."

"I know what an intercession is," Knox said, tightening his grip once more. "Tell me the target."

"Let me go and I will," the demon said.

"You don't belong here," Knox said.

"Come on," the demon said. "You know the only ones who visit this park are teenagers bent on drinking and smoking." Knox stood and shoved the demon away from him.

"Start talking, gout," Knox said. He checked his nose. The bleeding stopped.

"The name's Gad," the demon said, making a horrid attempt at a bow.

Knox twirled the dagger in his hand. "I don't care what your name is, slime. Tell me the mark or this dagger meets your brain."

"It's only rumors, but someone wants Drew Garrison for their collection," Gad said.

"Where have I heard that name?" Knox asked.

"He made the news last week when the cops found his work in a shallow grave," Gad said.

"Done," Knox said. "I'll do it."

Gad let out a joyful shriek.

"You think this is funny?" Knox sheathed the dagger. "You think murders are funny?"

Gad smirked. "I laugh because you think you're changing the world."

"I'll be changing *someone's* world," Knox said. "Who's the soul I'll be trading for?"

The demon shrugged. "No idea. Like I said, they're just whispers. Find Tartak after you get Drew. I'm sure he'll be able to point you in the right direction."

"Tartak and I aren't on the best terms," Knox said.

"I'm sure he could be persuaded," Gad said. "Good luck. And thanks for the deal."

Knox turned towards the nearest streetlight and walked away from the cacophony of children's laughter emanating from the playground.

KNOX BREATHED IN the stale air filling the police department. The noise and crowd at the precinct was perfect to blend in. He had scaled down his outfit, leaving his shotgun and revolver in his pickup truck, but kept the dagger with him. The metal detector wouldn't catch it.

"Can I see Drew Garrison?" Knox asked as he walked to the female officer behind the front desk.

The officer's face fell. "You another reporter? You don't look like one . . . ."

"Nope," he said. "I wanted to discuss a possible transfer."

"I didn't hear anything about that," the officer said and pursed her lips. "Let me get Captain Pearce up here. He can help you."

Knox walked to the side and leaned up against a wall in the main lobby. After a few minutes a serious looking man with a jet black mustache walked up to him. He wore a deep crease in the middle of his forehead.

"Afternoon. The name's Captain Pearce," he said as he chewed gum. "You a bounty hunter?"

"No. Right now I'm a liberator of sorts," Knox said.

Pearce groaned. "You're a bleeding heart defense attorney."

"I go by John Knox," Knox said as an idea sparked.

"What's this I hear about a transfer?" Pearce asked.

"I can't speak to that right now," Knox said. "Can I see Drew Garrison? Or is he not allowed to speak to attorneys?"

"Follow me," Pearce said plainly. Drew might be easier to grab than Knox originally thought. They exited the lobby and descended a staircase. "I've always wondered how you people can defend monsters like Drew."

"Everyone deserves to have his day in court. Before a judge," Knox added for good measure.

Pearce stopped and turned back at Knox so quick he thought the cop was going to hit him. "The man confessed to the murder. He killed his boy, for fuck's sake."

"His boy?" Knox asked. His posture went rigid. Gad hadn't mentioned anything about Drew murdering his son.

"Four years old," Pearce said. "We found his body badly bruised and burned. I had to send two of my officers to fucking therapy to cope with the incident."

"That's . . . I'm sorry," Knox said. His anger for Drew burned greater upon hearing the new information.

"Your firm not tell you that? You'll be defending a confessed child murderer," he said. "But what do you care? You're used to representing evil people."

"I don't represent evil," Knox said through gritted teeth.

"Who needs a trial?" Pearce stormed off. "I've got enough bullets in my service weapon."

"We'll need some privacy," Knox said as the two reached the end of the hallway. A thick steel door sat among a cement wall. Only through the tiny window in the door could Knox see a man sitting in the corner.

"Garrison, your lawyer's here," Pearce said. He turned to Knox. "I'm still cuffing him."

"Fine by me," Knox said.

Pearce pounded on the door. "Garrison, hands."

Drew walked up to them and put two gray hands through a slit in the door. Pearce clamped a pair of handcuffs on Drew's wrists.

"Back, Garrison," Pearce said. "Get back!" He opened the cell door.

Drew was a ghastly figure. He stood in a blue jumpsuit. His face sagged from depression and drugs. His short hair hung down over his forehead.

"That's not my attorney," Drew said.

"What?" Pearce asked. "What do you mean he's not—"

Knox brought a fist over the back of Pearce's head. The cop slumped to the floor. Knox sat Pearce upright against the wall and turned to Drew.

"You ready?" Knox asked.

"For what?" Drew asked.

"I'm getting you out of here," Knox said.

With a smirk, Drew walked over to Knox.

KNOX AND DREW cast a long shadow across the desert floor. Knox led Drew in iron shackles. The sun cursed them as they walked towards a small mound.

Knox knew the place well and hated it, but business was business. Gad let him know of an intercession, but not the place to exchange Drew nor the soul to be saved. So he traveled to the mound where Tartak lurked.

Before descending to the desert, Knox ensured he had all the proper provisions. His bandana protected his breathing. His clothes blended with the sand. Periodically he took a swig from the amber bottle in his hand. Its contents sent a shiver throughout his body.

"Keep it moving," Knox said.

Knox pulled Drew forward with every step. Drew's resemblance of a man began receding. Dirt caked his head and tears streamed down a contorted face. His shackles scored a cavern into his wrists, sending white lightning up his arms. He let out another wail.

"Shut it!" Knox barked. He whipped the chains forward again. The pleading moans tempted Knox to strike Drew dead on the spot.

"Why are you doing this? What'd I do to you?" Drew sobbed.

Knox pulled him forward again. "Murderers are always held

accountable." He huffed and stood tall, wrapping the irons around his forearm.

"I'm not a murderer," Drew said.

"I'm not your judge." Knox tugged the chains. "Now start cooperating."

Drew lurched forward. As he started in earnest, Knox yanked the chains, this time to send Drew to eat a mouthful of sand. When Drew thudded against the ground, he let out a whimper.

"Your life as a free man is over. Don't forget it." Knox tugged. "Now let's go. It's getting late."

Knox and Drew soon reached the mound. Loose dirt piled up to several times his height.

"Where are you taking me?" Drew asked.

Knox pulled him forward. "Tartak sits at the top of this."

"Who's Tartak?" Drew asked.

"Best to keep your balance here," Knox said, ignoring Drew's question. "I'll drag your ass up if you fall."

He and Drew struggled to climb the mound. Each step sent their feet into the dirt several inches. The loose dirt tumbled down behind them with each step.

When Knox made it to the top, he gave himself a moment's rest. The mound had plateaued to a flat sponge surface. He could see miles in each direction. Finally he reached down and pulled Drew up to him.

"Where's Tartak?" Drew asked.

"Must be hunting," Knox said, taking another swig from the bottle. Knox dropped Drew's chains and walked the perimeter of the plateau, but couldn't find Tartak. "Or he was hunted."

Knox grabbed his shotgun for peace of mind. He took another mouthful from the bottle and sprayed it on his arms.

"What are you—," Drew began.

Knox held up a finger. "You hear that?"

"No."

Knox felt a rumble through his feet, something that barely registered from the loose dirt. The sensation grew rapidly and shook his knees. Movement underneath!

Knox dropped the bottle. He pivoted and ran two steps.

The ground fell beneath him and a monstrosity erupted from below. A creature with fearsome mandibles and a dozen legs launched Knox into the air. He twirled helplessly as the dodecapede tracked his spiraling body.

The dodecapede caught Knox in its mouth. Knox grunted and fired his shotgun. The beast clamped harder and thrashed, and the shotgun slipped out of Knox's hands in the struggle. The dodecapede arced its back and swallowed Knox whole.

It dropped to all twelve legs and approached Drew. It chittered as it meandered across the plateau. Suddenly there was a muffled pop followed by a fleshy tear.

The dodecapede writhed and spun onto itself. It rolled on its back and swung its head into the dirt. Three more pops rang into the air, each louder than the last. More ripping echoed along the ridge followed by the monster's frantic behavior.

The dodecapede fell still onto its side. More ripping sounded and a flap of skin on its underside opened. Knox crawled out with his revolver in his left hand and his dagger in his right.

Knox walked over to his shotgun and plucked it from the dirt. He slung it over his back before grabbing Drew's chains and pulling him over to the dodecapede. Although motionless, the beast wheezed.

"We've been through this before, Tartak," Knox said, speaking in Tartak's native language. "If you spent half as much time learning to fight rather than coming up with new vices for humans, you'd have a chance at killing me."

"And if you keep on your current path, you'll end up here with me," Tartak said through its mandibles. "Your anger is consuming. It's no wonder you did a deal with Gad."

"I don't cut deals with demons," Knox said. He leveled his revolver at Tartak's thorax and pulled the trigger. The shot blasted the dodecapede's belly, sending shell and larvae everywhere.

"Okay," Tartak said. "What do you want?"

"If you've been talking with Gad, you know what I want," Knox said. "Where do I take this rat of a man?"

Tartak smiled. "The child murderer. Moloch will be pleased."

A chill trickled down Knox's spine. "Moloch? Gad never

mentioned anyone from the High Caste."

"Hope you can fight him like you can me," Tartak said.

Knox held up the amber bottle. "I've been drinking the blessings of a Southern preacher all day. Not many can touch me."

"We can smell you miles away," Tartak said.

"So where is he?" Knox asked.

"Keep heading into the desert," Tartak said. "You'll see an oasis."

"Till next time," Knox said. It had been the fourth time he'd incapacitated Tartak. Each time Tartak regenerated. As Knox yanked on Drew's chains, Knox wondered what their next encounter would look like.

KNOX'S BREATHING LABORED, his heart rate elevated after the encounter with Tartak. Growling set Knox on edge. Drew's face had twisted with his eyes blazing. Knox led him towards the oasis.

The oasis consisted of a wiry frame of palm trees and ash suspended in the air. An empty basin sat in the center. Inside, a leather ball rolled side to side.

Knox rested a hand on his revolver and descended. His stomach curled. Two demonic creatures formed the leathery ball. Their wings twitched every few moments accompanied with a shrill.

Knox stared at the abomination for a moment, anxiety forcing bile up his throat. He almost turned away, even, but one of the demons noticed him and stopped rolling. The larger one pulled away from its partner and stood tall. Even though he had not seen Moloch in a decade, his presence was unmistakable. Knox tightened his grip on the revolver's handle.

"Why are you here?" Moloch's voice was low and gravelly. As part of the High Caste, speaking in his native tongue gave him an advantage over humans.

"Good evening," Knox said in English, despite the sudden despair that threatened to overtake him. "You got some party."

The other demon fluttered over and grabbed Knox by the

collar. "Who are you to be intruding?"

Knox drew his pistol. A shot rang out. His aggressor lay on the ground, unconscious with a hole in his head.

"That's no way to treat Dagon." Moloch looked from his partner to Knox.

Knox rubbed his throat. "He'll be fine."

"You know, John," Moloch said, bending low, "I could destroy you for coming here. After all your tricks, all your deceptions."

"My deceptions?" Knox's eyes narrowed. "You followed the Father of Lies, Moloch. Not me."

"So?" Moloch asked, rubbing his chin with a scaled finger. "Why have you come bothering us here in the Pit?"

"I have a trade for you," Knox said. "Gad told me of an intercession for this worm." Knox tugged the chains.

Drew fell forward. He came at Knox, barking and thrashing. Knox backhanded him and sent him to the ground. When Drew scrambled to rise, Knox kicked him in the ribs. Drew squealed and retreated.

"Is this the child killer?" Moloch asked. His lips twisted into a smile as he grabbed Drew's face. Moloch pulled down Drew's jaw and inspected his mouth. "Such a great specimen."

"I figure a monster like you would appreciate this," Knox said.

"Oh, definitely," Moloch said. "Do you know the terror this will provide for my children?"

Knox swallowed hard. "Your children?"

"Surely my legacy endures on Earth," Moloch said. "You know, the unbaptized children."

"Shut it," Knox said. "Just give me the soul I saved."

"I don't think so," Moloch said. "I've got someone who needs to be reunited to his dear daddy." He snapped his fingers. A plume of dark smoke erupted behind him, revealing a blonde boy curled up on the ground. Tracks of burnt skin wrapped around his yellowed body.

"No," Knox said, becoming indignant. "You leave that boy alone. Give him to me."

"Andy," Moloch said in a sing-song voice. "Look who's

coming to live with you again."

Andy looked up at Knox, eyes darting towards Drew. "Daddy? Daddy . . . I'm scared."

"Enough, Moloch," Knox said. He felt hope fading. He had just delivered a torture device to a demon. "Give me the boy or I'll say the words of your Enemy."

"What of it?" Moloch asked, clearly irritated. "My Father can do that."

"I'll use his True Name," Knox responded.

"You don't know that."

"You wanna take that bet?"

"You'd be destroyed, annihilated."

"And you along with me."

Moloch hesitated before waving at Knox. "I don't want the kid anyways," Moloch said. "I have enough. Your gift pleases me well enough. Take his little runt."

"C'mon, kiddo," Knox said, motioning at Andy. "Let's go. Eyes on me. Let's leave this place." He knew that at any moment, Moloch might change his mind.

"What about Daddy?" Andy said when he reached Knox. "Can we take Daddy home? He didn't mean to hurt me."

Knox scooped Andy under his arm. He offered the child a drink from the amber bottle and it strengthened him. In a passing move, Knox glanced one last time at Drew. His eyes sunken and teeth bared, he now resembled an animal.

As Knox passed out of the oasis, he held his hands over Andy's ears so he wouldn't have to hear Drew's weeping and gnashing of teeth echo through the desert winds.

BACK IN LISLE, the night air hung silent on the playground. Knox walked through the park and only the jingle of his weapons could be heard in the darkness. The demon Gad hid above him in one of the trees.

"The intercession was completed," Knox said. Dry wings flapped in the dark. Suddenly Knox felt Gad nearby.

"See?" a voice called. Gad stepped into the glow of the nearby streetlight. "It all worked out in the end. I knew Moloch wouldn't be too much for you."

"See, I was wondering if you knew Moloch made the request," Knox said.

Gad shrugged. "I knew you would like our deal. You let me free, and I gave you information to save a kid."

"I told you before, Gad, that I don't do deals with demons." Knox drew his dagger and ran his fingers over the inscription. The dagger glowed.

"What's with the dagger?" Gad asked and took a step back.

Knox twirled it around in his hand. "Do you know why this blade is so effective against your race?"

"I don't really care," Gad said and fluttered back a few paces.

"It's inscribed with an ancient Greek word: *metanoia*," Knox said. He drew his pistol as Gad watched the blade.

"I'll see you around—"

Knox fired his revolver four times. Each time hit hard into Gad's wings. He fell to the ground and crawled along the grass. Gad tried to fly away but fell to the ground. Black blood oozed out of his wounds.

"It means 'repentance,' something your damned race is incapable of," Knox said and jumped on top of Gad. He dug his fingers into Gad's eyes and pulled his head back. "I told you before your kind didn't belong here."

Knox brought the dagger across Gad's throat and he turned to ash, dispelled back to the Pit. Knox stood and brushed himself off, walking towards the streetlight. He had a flight to Texas. There was a possessed man from Lubbock County that needed help.

**Adam Furman** lives in rural Illinois with his family of seven. He writes science fiction and fantasy, and his other work can be read in publications like *Broadswords & Blasters* and *EconoClash Review*. He successfully crowdfunded *Collateral Damage*, his kaiju/mech thriller, set for release in the Autumn of 2020. Sign up for his newsletter at <adamsfurman.com> or follow him on Twitter @AdamSFurman for updates.

**MISHA BURNETT**

# BAD DREAMS
# &
# BROKEN HEARTS

## THE CASE FILES OF ERIK RUGAR

"I don't know if what I did was right.
I'm not in the right-and-wrong business.
I am in the law-and-order business.
And all the kisses in the world won't change that."

*Truth and justice seldom travel the same roads.*

# The Unbroken Circle

## Victoria Weisfeld

ON A STIFLING Saturday morning in 1895, Ben Hooker, sheriff of Hendricks County, Indiana, was proved right again. Unlocking the office door, he'd said to his deputies, "Boys, the one thing about this goddam door is you never know what kind of goddam story will come busting through it." Then he propped the door open because the August heat wave was nowhere near breaking, and any whisper of a breeze was welcome. Not ten minutes later, in walked a local farmer carrying a story of murder.

"My name is William Bywater," said the stocky man, "and I've got a dead body in my front yard." He looked near thirty years of age, presentable. Prosperous even. Sober. That was a novelty.

"Who is it?" Sheriff Hooker asked.

"I don't know."

"Well, how'd he die? Or she?"

"The front of his shirt is a bloody mess."

"All right," said the sheriff. "Deputy Slade, write down the particulars."

Deputy Slade pulled a pad of paper out of a drawer and asked, "Where do you live, Mr. Bywater?"

"Near the National Road east of Stilesville."

The sheriff, confirming for the record, said, "So you never saw the dead man before?"

"No, sir. I saw him for the first time last night, and I don't mind telling you, he was an unwelcome visitor."

The sheriff indicated a chair in front of his desk, and Deputies Slade and Turner pulled their chairs around to hear what William Bywater had to say.

William and his wife Lillie were hosts of his family's annual reunion. By Friday afternoon late, everyone had arrived. After supper, three generations of Bywater siblings and cousins, parents and children—forty-five people in all—gathered in a

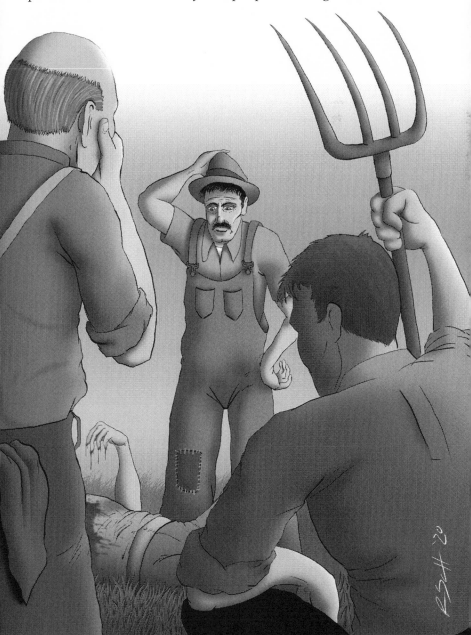

large circle around a few burning logs. They sat in chairs and on blankets, some stood, and others were perched on flatbed wagons filled with hay.

As William described it, he built the fire more for light than warmth. The applewood logs smelled good too. Maybe because of the crackling fire or the crowd's excited rustling, William said, no one noticed the approaching stranger until a tall, gaunt-featured man split their tight circle like a break in a wagon wheel that, even mended, might never again run as smooth. His hands and face were rough and sun-weathered, and his travel-worn clothes drooped from skinny shoulders, as beat-up and dirty as his hat.

The sheriff asked, "This the man now lying dead in your yard?"

William nodded, then described how the intruder stepped uninvited into the firelight and said, "Got somethin for you."

To which William replied, "All right, mister. I'm William Bywater. This is my family, and this is my farm. Have you had your supper?"

"I'll not be taking any of your food," he said.

"All right then. What do you have for us?"

"Please, here's a chair." William's wife Lillie pushed the kitchen chair she'd occupied toward the man, but he continued standing.

"Who's the oldest man here?" he said.

"I am," said Grandpa John, William's father.

"Then this is yours," the stranger said. A flickering smile that William said might have been a trick of the light touched the man's face. He reached into his leather knapsack and pulled out a Bible. Thick, folio-sized, with a tooled cover and gilt-edged pages.

William's sister Molly flew across the circle to the man's side. "Good heavens! Our Bible!"

William told the sheriff how Molly had been entrusted with the family Bible when their mother died. But the previous year, when she moved to Broad Ripple to teach, the Bible disappeared. It was a loss to all of them, because the pages bound into the book between the old and new testaments, recorded generations of Bywater family births, marriages, and deaths.

John Bywater squinted at the stranger, then said, "Thank you, mister." He received the thick Bible in both hands. "How'd you come by it?"

The man said he found it in Springfield, Ohio, in the trash from a bankrupt general store. William said, "He saw the most recent child was born near Stilesville. That would be my daughter, Celia. 'As I'm headed west,' he said, 'I could deliver it, and here I be.' Then he limped toward the road."

The sheriff turned to his deputies. "This man fit the description of any of those characters we're watching out for?"

"Not a one," said Deputy Turner.

"Go on," the sheriff said to William.

The stranger disappeared into the evening gloom and out of the family's thoughts and the Family History Circle commenced.

"How many people you have there again?" the sheriff asked.

"Nineteen adults and twenty-six children."

Sheriff Hooker chuckled. "Your wife has more forbearance than mine."

"She wasn't best pleased I volunteered to have the reunion at our farm without asking her first," William admitted. "These past weeks Lillie tore through the house puffing like a steam engine and twice as hot."

"I know ma will ask me," said Deputy Slade. "How d'you feed all them people?"

"Our farm has loads of sweet corn and beans. We butchered a hog. And my relatives brought bacon and hams, fruits and vegetables, chickens. We have our own chickens and geese. Ducks too. They brought fresh-baked bread, fruit pies, and store-bought groceries from Indianapolis."

The sheriff said, "That's an impressive undertaking, but it's not why you're here."

"No. The trouble started after the Family History Circle, when we got a look at the Bible."

It was late when they got the kids bedded down in the barn and hay wagons, William said, the parents taking turns in the night to check on them. Lillie lit oil lamps in the kitchen. The adults gathered around the big table, eager to reacquaint themselves with the Bible's family register. Its entries spanned generations and were written by many hands.

Alongside some of the names were new notations. Molly gasped when she saw the first of these, and angry muttering broke out.

"When we realized what those additions were about, I closed the book and said we'd had enough for one night," William said.

"Go on," the sheriff said, hoping the dead body would appear soon. People needed to tell a story in their own way, and he generally didn't try to hurry them. They just looped back to what they planned to say in the first place anyway.

"Early the next morning, Grandpa Pete was on his way to the outhouse and saw something in the front yard, near the road. When he went to investigate, he found the dead man. He came in the house and got me, and I got my two brothers, and we went to see. There was that stranger, lying on his side, with a great bloody spot on his shirt-front.

"Lillie brought out an old blanket, and we laid it over him so people on the road couldn't gawk and to keep the flies off. His horse was tied to a tree, and my brother Lewis brought it hay and a pail of water. I saddled my horse and headed to Danville to get you."

"And nobody in the family knows who the dead man was?"

"No, I guess. For certain, I never saw him before."

Before the sheriff left his office, he told Deputy Turner to call up the coroner in Indianapolis and suggest he recruit a couple of local doctors to help examine the body, then bring a wagon to Bywater's farm.

SHERIFF HOOKER, DEPUTY Slade, and Bywater had an hour's ride in front of them. To pass the time, the sheriff said, "Tell us more about the Family History Circle you had last night. What is that?"

William said it started with his great-great grandparents, as a way to pass on the family's history to the younger generation. "Each year we retell the family stories from the time the first Bywaters came to America, up to the current day, though our more recent history is pretty tame after the sea voyages, Indian raids, witch trials, and wars.

"We settled first in New England, relocated to North Carolina in the 1700s. Revolutionary War veterans received bounty lands in Tennessee, and we moved again. The current family elders—brothers John and Pete, and their late brother Spencer—lived in Tennessee for many years. Spencer died in the Civil War. After the war, their farms were floundering, and we moved to central Indiana. Now some of us are moving from our farms into the big city."

"Indianapolis?"

"Yes, sir."

They reached the farm around ten in the morning, and found one of William's brothers sitting in a chair by the body. William introduced him, saying, "This here's Jake, my oldest brother. Then in the middle is Lewis. Short and stocky like me. And here comes my wife Lillie. You should know her too."

"And our dad, Grandpa John," Jake said.

"And his brother, Grandpa Pete."

"And our sister, Molly."

"Whoa, whoa," Sheriff Hooker said. "I'll do my best." Stepping to the blanket-covered body, he said, "Let's see what we have here."

Tall as Sheriff Hooker was, Jake was taller and thin as a pencil. He had to fold in thirds to help remove the blanket. Just as William said, the dead man lay on his side, his shirt well bloodied and marred with scorch-marks. His trouser knees were grass-stained, and the sheriff conjectured he'd collapsed to his knees, fallen on his side, and bled to death on the spot.

The sheriff turned the body onto its back and opened his long coat to examine his pockets. He found papers identifying the bearer as Jacob Sinclair, including a letter offering him a job as horse-trainer at the Four-Cornered Track in Terre Haute.

"He was headed that direction," William said. "Said he was going west."

About that time, Deputy Turner arrived, driving a wagon.

With help from a couple of Bywater men, the sheriff and his deputies loaded the body into the wagon and, the day being hot, Deputy Turner turned the horses toward Indianapolis without delay.

While Deputy Slade ambled about the yard and outbuildings, Sheriff Hooker addressed the adults ranged in the shade of the big oak tree. They looked stunned by the calamity. "Did all of you see the stranger last night?"

Nods and murmurs of agreement.

"Who was he?" Lillie asked.

"It appears his name was Jacob Sinclair. Did any of you know him? Recognize him?"

Grandpa Pete said, "Sinclair? Some Sinclairs lived in our part of Tennessee. We weren't friendly with them, though."

"I remember the family," said William's brother Jake. "The Sinclair kids were hellions."

Grandpa John said, "Now you say that, Pete, he did look a mite familiar. But at my age, everybody reminds me of somebody."

"I won't say it, but your eyes aren't what they used to be, either," Pete added.

"Had a hard life, from the looks of him," the sheriff said.

They nodded. "Down and out," Jake said.

"His horse seems healthy, though, and he had money on him," the sheriff said. "Did anyone hear anything last night, when checking on the children, for instance?"

Again, no.

"And he didn't put up a fight," the sheriff said. "No injuries to his hands or forearms." He raised his arms to show how a man might try to defend himself. "The body was just starting to stiffen up—pardon me, ladies—so I'd say he was killed around four or five in the morning. Any idea why he was here at that time?"

"No, sir," said several, in a shudder of shaking heads.

"Our children sleep outside in the wagons at night, sheriff," William said, and asked the logical next question. "D'you think the murderer might come back?"

"That's a good one, and I don't have the answer," the sheriff said. "Judging by how vicious the attack was, I'd be inclined to say it was personal, but I just don't know."

The sheriff sent Deputy Slade back to the office while he interviewed each of the couples separately in the front parlor of the farmhouse, starting with William and Lillie. He perched on a settee that seemed too flimsy for his bulk, while they sat in chairs.

"Since he didn't want any supper," Lillie said, "I figured he might have had a meal somewhere close by. Maybe wherever he asked directions to our farm."

"An interesting assumption, ma'am," the sheriff said. "We'll look into it." Then he said, "All the adults saw the Bible Sinclair brought, is that right?"

"Yes," William said.

"I suppose the Bible entries captured everyone's attention pretty well," the sheriff said. "I'm having a little trouble understanding how they were changed."

"Well, here." William fetched the thick Bible and laid it atop a low table, positioning it in front of the settee. He riffled the thin pages until he found the one headed "Deaths," and pointed to an entry.

"This is my Uncle Spencer, who died in the War. His widow and two children and their kids are here at the farm." William's voice was barely audible. "Aunt Louise probably still has the letter from his commanding officer, saying what a fine soldier he was."

"Uh-huh," the sheriff said, a variant on "Go on."

"See here, someone wrote 'Matt. 24:10.'" Seeing the sheriff's puzzlement, he added, "It's a Bible verse."

"I'm afraid I don't—"

Lillie intoned, *"And then shall many be offended, and shall betray one another, and shall hate one another."* Lillie studied the back of her chapped hands. "My father was a Baptist preacher."

"What do you make of it?" the sheriff asked.

"I don't know what to make of it," William said. "It's that word 'betray.' We always thought—think—of Spencer as a family hero."

"Is somebody's saying he wasn't?" Sheriff Hooker scratched behind his ear. He pointed to another entry. "Name, death date, and another Bible verse, I reckon?"

"Yes," Lillie said, craning to see where the sheriff pointed. "Lewis Bywater was William's grandfather. He scrimped and saved to buy this farm after the War. When he finally got it, it felt like a miracle." She faltered.

"'Ex. 20:15.' 'Ex.' is Exodus, I presume."

"You should know this one, sheriff. *Thou shalt not steal.*"

William paced the room. He said, "When we saw that, we were dumbfounded. Read the one by my Dad's birth."

It was I Cor. 6:8. Lillie turned to the verse and read, "*Nay, ye do wrong, and defraud, and that your brethren.* Sheriff, John Bywater is the most upright man I've ever met, my own pastor father not excepted. It made me furious." Lillie's eyes flashed, and William reached over to take her hand.

Sheriff Hooker pursed his lips. "And you think Jacob Sinclair added these scurrilous references? Just because they're in the Bible doesn't mean they apply to your family. These words are thousands of years old."

Lillie responded sadly. "But they do plant a worm of doubt to gnaw at our hearts and our regard for each other. *And thy life shall hang in doubt before thee; and thou shalt fear day and night, and shalt have none assurance of thy life.* Deuteronomy 28:66."

William said, "If he found the Bible at a general store like he claimed, someone else could have had it before him, and that person could have written these slanders. But why?"

That was not a question Sheriff Hooker could answer. Nor could any of the other family members he talked with afterward.

Last interviewed was William's oldest brother Jake and his wife. When they entered the front parlor, Sheriff Hooker was studying the marriage entry for Jake's parents, John Bywater and Lucy Fort. He met Jake's eyes. "Ezek. 16:15 is written by your mother's name. I read it." He replayed the verse in his mind: *But thou didst trust in thine own beauty, and playedst the harlot because of thy renown, and pouredst out thy fornications on every one that passed by; his it was.* "Pretty rough. You're her oldest child, correct?"

"Yes," Jake rasped.

The Sheriff turned to the "Births" pages. "Here you are, born but eight months after the wedding. Deuteronomy 23:2: *A bastard shall not enter into the congregation of the Lord; even to his tenth generation.* What do you make of it?"

"Can't make heads nor tails of it." Jake studied his boots.

The sheriff took a gamble. "Says here your name is 'Jacob S. Bywater.' What's the 'S' stand for? Not Jacob Sinclair Bywater, I hope."

Jake slammed out of the room and stalked off toward the barns. His tearful wife watched him go. She said, "Jake's mother told him who his father was on her deathbed. She said none of the boys know. Not Grandpa John neither." She twisted her wedding ring around and around. "Jacob Sinclair took her by force, and she was too ashamed and frightened to tell anyone. She and John were already engaged and married right away, which was fortunate because she was with child. Women take the blame, you know, sheriff, regardless of the circumstances."

Sheriff Hooker nodded, well aware of the cruel assumptions people made, the indelible stain on a woman's reputation, and the impact they have. He'd seen the guilt up close. Fractured marriages, suicides, abandoned babies.

"She gave Jake that name as a constant reminder to shun sin and as penance for deceiving Grandpa John. But it wouldn't surprise me if that secret was one reason she died before her time."

"How did Jake react?"

"He hates his name now. Yet, to him, it was all a lifetime ago, far away in Tennessee. He never thought it would touch us in the here and now. Best he could do was respect her secret."

And his own, the sheriff thought. Jake isn't a Bywater after all.

"You won't say anything?"

Ben Hooker didn't make promises he couldn't keep, even about a third-hand rumor. "Not unless I have to."

He rode home with the heavy Bible in his saddlebag,

and a heavier heart. Either the Bywater family had erected a respectable but false front, or someone had concocted a devious plot against them.

IN THE OFFICE the next morning, Deputy Turner reported in. "There were some clothes and such in Sinclair's saddlebags, and the coroner found this." He handed over a small black notebook. "Full of numbers. Maybe you can make it out."

"Go on," the sheriff said, flipping through pages.

"Two doctors examined the body with him. A stab wound to the chest killed him and caused all the blood."

"Knife?"

"Not a pocket-knife. A big one with a six or seven-inch blade."

Turner added, "Seeing him laid on the table, naked like that—" As he recalled the scene, the color went out of his face, and his eyes threatened to roll up in his head. Sheriff Hooker grabbed his arm and settled him in a chair.

"And as we saw, his shirt was scorched, and the hair on his chest. There'll be an inquest for sure."

"Time of death?"

"Early Saturday morning, between, say, three and six," Turner said, breathing deeply, collecting himself.

"Like you thought, sheriff," Slade said.

"Let's assume he was at the farm by four in the morning. You need to find out where he was before then, after he left the farm Friday evening," the sheriff said "Today's Sunday. Most people will be home after church. You deputies go into Stilesville and knock on doors. See if anyone saw him or any stranger, for that matter. Could be someone killed Sinclair then went on their way. Course, if he's hiding out in Marion County, he'll be hard to find. Too many damn people."

"Does Stilesville have a hotel?" Slade asked. "It's on the National Road."

"There might be a rooming house or tavern where travelers can put up for the night. See what you can find."

"Are you thinking someone from the family killed him?" Slade asked. "That might explain why he didn't call out to them."

"Why didn't he call out even if it *was* one of them?" asked Turner.

"Interesting," said the sheriff. "About the family, then. They are deeply attached to their family history, that's for damn sure. I studied more on those Bible verses last night. I got the impression that whoever took note of them had only a passing understanding of how some of them fit into more complicated stories. Not what someone who really knows their Bible would do. A damn trickster, is what I think."

"Why was Sinclair at the farm?" Slade said. "All the blood on the ground means he was killed right there. It's not like he went back for help or anything."

"I don't know," the sheriff said, "but if I had to guess, I'd say he wanted something."

"Was he planning to blackmail them to keep the family secrets?" Slade asked.

The sheriff chewed his lip, then said, "Are the secrets implied by the Bible verses even worth anything? I'm inclined to believe they were more mean than true. The only ones with some evident truth to them have to do with Jake Bywater not being Grandpa John's son. His mother told him as much when she was dying."

"I almost forgot," Deputy Slade said. He picked up a something long and thin as a yardstick wrapped in dirty canvas and leaning against the wall. He unrolled it on the floor and the three men stared. It was a long stick with a dirty rag wrapped around one end, like a torch.

"What is it?" the sheriff asked.

"When you sent me out to walk the property, I found this near the barn. There was a scorched place on the ground where it was, and the grass around it was all beaten down, like it had been stomped on."

"Maybe they put out torches at night, to light the kids' way to bed," Turner said.

"Unwrap that cloth there at the top."

When he did, the underneath layers revealed cloth in a blue-and-white checkered pattern. "What's that remind you of?"

the sheriff asked.

"Sinclair's shirt," Slade said.

"And the spare shirt in his saddlebag," Turner added. "Maybe somebody caught him trying to set fire to the barn."

"That would be awful, if true."

THE CORONER'S JURY heard testimony from the sheriff, the deputies, and the doctors who examined the body, as well as William Bywater. The owner of a Stilesville tavern told them Sinclair took his dinner after eight o'clock that Friday night, then went up to one of her upstairs rooms, to sleep, she supposed. He went out again in the middle of the night. She thought he went to the outhouse, but fell back asleep and didn't hear him return. Although the jury came to the obvious conclusion that Jacob Sinclair was murdered, none of the evidence pointed to any particular assailant.

The county prosecutor, eager to glean a court case out of the matter, hounded Sheriff Hooker. Meanwhile, the sheriff's hopes were pinned on the response to a letter he'd sent the sheriff of Wilson County, Tennessee.

He'd also written to the Four-Cornered Track in Terre Haute advising them of their would-be employee's death and asking what his duties would have been. The track manager responded, saying they took Sinclair on because they needed another horse trainer. He said Sinclair hoped to buy and sell horses, though he scoffed at that notion. "Takes a lot more cash than he'll make here, but I let him think he could try."

The track manager was right. As best the sheriff could interpret the figures in Sinclair's diary, he needed a considerable sight more money than he had to get a foothold in that business. And, apparently, he had no way to get it— legally, that is.

In late September, the response arrived from Wilson County, its tardiness attributable to the rigor with which the Tennessee sheriff had tackled Sheriff Hooker's questions. He'd interviewed numerous people—pastors, merchants, long-time residents, and teachers at the school the Bywater and Sinclair children attended.

That information, along with his own recollections, led Sheriff Bond to conclude that the Sinclair family was "mean as snakes," and he provided several vivid examples. Poorer than most, the Sinclairs—adults and children alike—were not well regarded. "My wife was a teacher," he wrote, "and she dreaded having one of the little varmints in her classroom."

Another teacher recalled an incident involving her close friend Mrs. John Bywater, the former Lucy Fort. Touched by the raggedy condition of the Sinclair children (who went to school barefoot until snow was on the ground), she proposed to give them her children's few outgrown garments and asked the teacher to deliver them. She wouldn't take them herself because, she said, "I know they can be touchy."

Arriving at the Sinclair cabin, the teacher encountered Jacob Sinclair. When he realized who the donation came from, he pushed her out the door. "We don't need a whore's charity," he shouted and more words to that effect. As the teacher grabbed the basket of clothes, he put his face in hers, yelling, "Take that filthy harlot's rags right back to her!" The scandalized teacher was still shaking when she described the encounter to Lucy.

Over the years, the Wilson County sheriff reported, the Sinclair children scattered. Their family owned no property; there was nothing to keep them. A married daughter moved to Ohio, one son was in prison, and their sharp-tongued mother died a year or so back. The family patriarch disappeared shortly thereafter, though the sheriff wasn't sure exactly when. Old Jacob Sinclair preferred horses to people, and it took a while for his former neighbors to realize he was gone.

"To sum up," Sheriff Bond wrote, "the Sinclairs were the opposite of the Bywater family in every respect: schooling, church attendance, cleanliness, hard work, and prosperity, at least until the War, when every citizen of this county suffered mightily."

Sheriff Hooker leaned back in his chair and folded his arms across his chest. An hour later Deputy Slade returned from checking on the report of a barn broken into and found him deep in thought.

"Maybe I've been in this job too long," he told Slade. "Everybody's supposed to get justice through our legal system. But sometimes it arrives in other ways."

"Huh?"

Then he wrote another letter.

The response to this letter soon arrived, because Hooker asked the Tennessee sheriff only one question. Yes, Sheriff Bond wrote, the Sinclair daughter's in-laws knew where she lived now and provided an address in Springfield, Ohio.

"Springfield," Slade said. "Isn't that where Sinclair said he found the Bible?"

"Sure is. Clark County. And I know their sheriff."

Sensing he was closing in on something, Hooker took a chance on a telegram. In a couple of days, he received a letter in response. Jacob Sinclair had roosted with Annie Sinclair Dodson for about six months earlier that year.

The Clark County sheriff asked Annie whether her father had a big Bible, and she described the Bywater Bible to a T. He asked how Jacob came by it, and she "hemmed and hawed," finally admitting he'd stolen it "from some gal in Indiana." When the sheriff told her about Jacob Sinclair's murder, Annie, far from grief-stricken, said, "I told him his Bible study—reading all day, writing down verses—wouldn't do him no good. He was a bad un, first to last."

BEN HOOKER ARRIVED at the Bywater farm around lunchtime. Lillie was in the kitchen, slicing vegetables with a sturdy knife, while four-year-old Celia played on the floor with her doll. In a few minutes, William came in, hot and dusty, and his wife handed him a cup of water.

"Hey, sheriff," he said.

"William. I have news."

Lillie glanced at Celia, but the sheriff said, "She can stay. Based on my investigations, I do believe Jacob Sinclair stole your Bible and made those notations. He took it in the confusion of your sister's move, which suggests he was keeping an eye on your family members, at least some of the time.

"He knew your family back in Tennessee and harbored a grudge against the Bywaters. More prosperous, well-regarded, as his family was not. A certain kind of man can never let that stuff go.

"When he messed with those Bible pages, he was trying to hurt you the only way he knew how. I'm told your Family History Circles were well known in Wilson County. What you consider your strength, he saw as weakness. A cloud of suspicion could poison your good opinion of the family, past and present. It would do his destructive work for him, from within. He wouldn't have to lift a finger against you."

"What a despicable man," Lillie said.

After a pause, the sheriff said, "Just speculate here a minute. How far would Bywater go to protect the family? To quench any unsavory rumors?"

"You mean that Jake isn't our father's son?" William asked.

The sheriff raised an eyebrow.

"We've suspected that for years. He doesn't look anything like the rest of us, for one thing. No one ever dared say it to Jake's face, though. I suppose what you're getting around to is that Jacob Sinclair was his father."

Hooker kept quiet.

"Sheriff, not one of us Bywaters would go two steps out of our way to harm an old liar like Jacob Sinclair. But every one of us would go to the ends of the earth to protect our brother."

"And protect your kids, I suppose."

The knife fell from Lillie's hand and clattered into the sink.

Sheriff Hooker sighed. "I guess we'll never know who killed the old coot." Lillie set a steaming plate in front of him. "My, Lillie, you've outdone yourself."

**Vicki Weisfeld's** short stories have appeared in *Sherlock Holmes Mystery Magazine*, *Mystery Weekly*, and *Ellery Queen Mystery Magazine*; "Breadcrumbs" won a 2017 Derringer Award. Find her work in the anthologies Busted: Arresting Stories from the Beat, *Seascapes: Best New England Crime Stories*, *Murder Among Friends*, *Passport to Murder*, *The Best Laid Plans*, *Quoth the Raven*, and *Sherlock Holmes in the Realms of Edgar Allan Poe*. Online: <vweisfeld.com> and book reviews at the UK website <crimefictionlover.com>.

*Look to the refined for the most
primitive secrets of all.*

# How to Make a Boulevardier

## Nils Gilbertson

THE FIRST TIME Lucy came over to the house in tears and
spoke with Mom in private, no one thought too much of it.
It was a little odd, though. Mom ushered Lucy into her office
behind heavy, oak doors. P.J. and Big Al, our security, stood
by with their arms crossed like a couple of washed-up secret
service goons. It was all standard routine when Mom had
a meeting.

Mom headed the family business since Dad was killed
a couple of years ago. Bill and I took on officer roles. Bill
was older and did most of the heavy lifting. He was born
for business and he knew it. Ever since he was in the third
grade and conned little Melvin Cartwright into trading his
sour candies for an expired milk box, he thought he could
sell earplugs to the deaf. But, being a Gray, he didn't end
up with an MBA and a marketing gig. Nope. Grays don't
go for dull lives like that. Instead, he was busy deciding
which gubernatorial candidate would be the most "business"
friendly. He was negotiating deals for distribution chains
throughout the Midwest, and we weren't distributing
breakfast cereal or stereo equipment. When negotiations broke
down, he was at the warehouse on the cold, grim outskirts
of town with P.J. and Big Al resorting to less subtle forms of
persuasion. He was damn good at it. But, Bill was the sort
of guy that thought if you're good at one thing, you're good
at everything. And if you get away with one crime, you're
bulletproof. He was that special sort of stupid.

If you ask me, a smart man knows his strengths and sticks to them. So, I hung around the house, entertained guests, and fixed cocktails. Mom always said I was squandering my potential. Truth is I didn't think much of some of our operations. Not like I was a self-righteous type, but some ventures pushed the boundary on what I considered morally acceptable. I couldn't quite articulate my reasons, so I never brought it up with anyone. But deep in my gut, some things didn't feel right. Maybe morals come from the gut and not the head. Hell, who am I to talk about morals. Still, it bothered me. So I figured if I played the limited role of bartender and wisecrack, I'd limit my culpability.

Speaking of limiting culpability, our younger sister Leanne didn't have much interest in the whole thing. She pulled her weight by marrying an accountant, Herb. Turns out, having an accountant at our fingertips came in handy. Even though she wasn't part of our operations, she was still around. In the Gray family, no one got far.

After decades of building it up through keen business savvy, friends and family in high places, and a few broken arms and bloody noses—or worse—there was little distinguishing between the Gray family and the Gray business. When Mom and Dad had kids, we inherited it. And boy what a business it was. No matter who you were in the city—politician, judge, cop, CEO—you didn't get where you wanted to without the Grays. And you didn't get through the Grays without disappearing for a meeting behind the heavy, oak doors, P.J. and Big Al standing guard. So when Lucy burst into the house, giving us little more than a nod, trying to hide her mascara-stained cheeks, escaping behind the office doors, it was a little odd.

BILL MARRIED LUCY when they were eighteen. She and Bill were inseparable from the ripe age of five. By fifteen, they were going to high school dances together, and by eighteen, ready to tie the knot. By thirty, they had a small army of kids. That's how Mom and Dad liked it. If one of us brought someone new home, it caused more paranoia than a house of mirrors full of schizophrenics. So nothing could've been better than the oldest Gray marrying a girl who was one of our own. A little incestuous, but safe.

Bill was a good talker, but Lucy was the thinker. Behind closed doors, she was pulling strings. I couldn't scrub from my mind the scene in high school when some nameless oaf dared to hold the door open for Lucy and told her she looked pretty as a movie star. That afternoon she feigned offense to Bill and me. The next day after class, his hand was duct-taped to the football field goalpost and Bill was smashing it to bits with his helmet. Lucy watched and giggled while the kid's bones crunched and he wailed like a hog in the scalding tank. I watched and did nothing. I was only a kid, but it's the kind of thought that creeps in and twists your gut decades later. I remember the sounds.

That first time Lucy hustled into Mom's office, crying, we didn't make much of it. But then it happened a second time— and a third. Bill was never around during the meetings, which caught my attention.

After the fourth meeting, I decided to inquire. I was in the dining room beginning to fix a Negroni but decided to fix a Boulevardier instead. It was getting deep into the fall season and replacing the gin with rye gave the cocktail a certain coziness. The familiar burn of the whiskey, bolstered by the sweetness of the vermouth and the bitterness of the Campari made consciousness feel like home—especially on a brisk fall evening, yellow and orange leaves swirling in the crisp breeze before landing gently on the lawn outside.

A short hallway separated the dining room from the office. Mom knocked from the inside of the door and P.J. opened it for her. I glanced down the hall. Lucy walked out like her muscles were lead. She wasn't crying, but her face ached with the exhaustion of grief. Mom whispered something to her. Lucy nodded and went out the back door with P.J. and Big Al onto the sprawling plot of land that was the backyard.

Mom walked towards the dining room and I turned back to the bar.

"Can I fix you something?"

"What're you making?"

"Boulevardier," I said. "But I can make anything you like."

"I'll do a gin and tonic."

"Always one for the classics. Hey Mom?"

"Yes, Joseph?" She took her seat at the head of the dining room table.

"Was that Lucy in there again?"

"Yes."

"On business?"

She turned and looked at me. "Why're you so keen on knowing what's going on with Lucy?"

"Thought I could help is all."

"If I need your help, you'll know about it."

"Okay." I went on fixing the drinks. There was no point pressing for more information. If Mom wanted us to know something, we knew it. If she didn't, we didn't. I topped the gin with tonic water and went to the kitchen for a lime. When I came back she was staring at the empty chair opposite her, where Dad used to sit.

I garnished her drink and served it. "Here you go. I used gin from Uncle Rick's distillery, just how you like."

"Thank you. Joseph?"

"Yeah?"

"I didn't mean to be short with you about Lucy. I know I've been pushing for you to take on a bigger role, and you were only trying to help. You'll know about Lucy as soon as there is anything worth knowing."

"Sure, Mom."

THE COCKTAILS HAD me buzzed so I went into the backyard. The cold burn of the wind on my cheeks and nose and ears brought life. I walked down the path that meandered through a patch of walnut trees, the naked branches like gnarled fingers. I made my way to the family cemetery at the back corner of the property. Lucy was standing with P.J. and Big Al, looking at the family gravestones, Dad's—the most recent—in the front corner.

When I joined them, P.J. and Big Al nodded at me and

turned back towards the house. I examined my sister-in-law. There were traces of utter despair on her face, but it was muted by a new look of raw determination.

"I bet you still aren't used to the graves in the backyard," I said.

She smiled faintly. "I've been running around this yard for almost as long as you have, Joe."

"I guess that's right. I'm not sure I'm used to them." The wind rustled the trees. "We didn't even have a proper funeral back here when Dad died, remember? One day, there was a gravestone."

"There was nothing to put in the ground," she mumbled.

I swallowed the brick in my throat. I recalled the day a couple of years back when Dad went missing for a few days and then we received a letter in the mail with GPS coordinates. Below an out of use, rusting water tower, there was a large brown bag. In it, a box of bone fragments and a container of puke green sludge. There was a note that said: DON'T BOTHER WITH A DNA TEST—IT'S HIM. It took some egghead professor from the local college to convince us the killer wasn't some body-dismembering sorcerer. Instead, whoever it was had access to a fancy cremation machine that turns dead bodies to untraceable gook. The professor also told us the remains made great fertilizer. I have to give it to Dad, Mom's garden looked great that spring.

I pushed it to the back of my mind next to Bill's helmet swings.

"Are you all right, Lucy?"

She looked at me like it'd be the last time we ever see each other and she was getting a good look so if we met again she'd remember. "I will be."

I nodded and scanned the graves. I noticed Great Aunt Sheila's—next to Dad's—was scarred at the corner like someone had been stabbing at it.

We stood in silence for a few minutes and she said, "Want to go inside? It's getting cold."

A FEW DAYS later Bill stopped by the house. He hadn't been around recently but I figured he'd been off somewhere on business. I was in the living room reading when he came by. The top button of his crisp, light blue dress shirt was undone and his tie loosened. It was spattered red. He came in, skulking around the place like some sort of burglar. I sat watching him for a few moments before he noticed me.

"Hell, Joe, you startled me."

"You're the one bursting in here."

"Right. You see Lucy around?"

"Nope."

"How 'bout Mom?"

"Sure. Mom lives here."

"I know she lives here. I mean have you seen her recently?"

"How recently?"

Bill lifted his arms, annoyed. "I don't know, an hour?"

"Nope. You want a drink? I've been making Boulevard–"

"No thanks. How about some water?"

"You can get your water."

Bill walked into the kitchen and I followed him. "Hey Bill, there's blood on your shirt."

"Huh?" He looked down. "Shit."

"You been busy these days? Are you negotiating a deal? Guns? Pills?

"No, I–" He paused. "Yeah. I've been out in Des Moines working on some things."

"Wow, sure sounds exciting. Mom hasn't told me about that."

Bill took a sip of water and put a hand on my shoulder. "Look, Joe, truth is Mom doesn't tell you about much. I wish things were different. There sure is enough work to go around, especially come election season next year. We got people to scrutinize. But Mom doesn't feel comfortable with you taking the lead on that sort of thing."

I looked him in the eye. I thought about telling him about Lucy being around. Before I could make up my mind he started again. "How about this, I'll talk to Mom about expanding your role, yeah?"

"Sure, Bill."

"Great." He looked at his watch. "I've got to pick the kids up from soccer. Can I borrow a shirt?"

THE NEXT MORNING I found an envelope at the base of my bedroom door saying that Mom called a special family meeting for the following evening. It was sort of funny that P.J. still went around delivering the handwritten notices to everyone. You'd think by now we'd have an email group or something.

I didn't think much about the subject matter; special meetings weren't exactly out of the ordinary. Mom was good about calling them when big issues were at stake. She was pretty democratic like that. Instead, I thought it would be nice to reach out to everyone beforehand and have a drink ready at each seat. If it was a serious matter, we all could use a stiff one before.

I ran into Mom as I headed downstairs for breakfast.

"Morning, Mom."

"Morning, Joseph."

"I was thinking about asking around before the meeting tomorrow night to get drink orders."

She frowned. "It's not a social club."

"I know, but they'll be nice drinks."

She sighed. "Okay, reach out to your Uncle Vin, I'm sure he'll want something. And Leanne. Don't bother with Bill, Lucy, or me."

"Lucy's coming?"

"Sure, she's part of the family isn't she?"

"Yeah, she doesn't always come is all."

Mom walked off into the kitchen for breakfast.

I followed and watched her at the table. I could tell she was thinking things over. She was always the thinker in the family. Dad got things done. Like Bill, but without the air of false accomplishment. He built it and it humbled him. He never passed up a chance to get his hands dirty—or bloody—though. He said it was a matter of honor. He didn't want to stand by like some white-collar prick while his guys were cracking jaws. The older I got the more I wondered whether it was honor or bloodlust. Maybe honor is bloodlust dressed up nice.

I recalled Mom's reaction to Dad's murder. If it were

the other way, he'd have graduated from run-of-the-mill organized criminal to supervillain. But Mom was calm. She said to find who did it, we had to expand our influence, and we did. But, we never found which of Dad's enemies was responsible. And Mom wasn't one to guess wrong and bring hell down on the rest of us.

That afternoon, I called Uncle Vin, Uncle Irv, and Leanne. Uncle Vin said he'd have three fingers of the best scotch I had, neat. Irv chuckled and reminded me he was eight years sober. I felt stupid for forgetting. I offered to come up with some sort of mocktail but he wasn't having it. Leanne wanted a glass of white wine. The drink orders disappointed me. I decided to have the ingredients ready to whip up a couple of extra Boulevardiers in case someone tried mine and liked it.

IRV WAS THE first to show the following evening. He was a fat, bald man that always gave you a squeeze when you saw him. I went out and greeted him on the front porch and he damn near picked me up off the ground.

"Little Joe!" He took a step back and looked me up and down. "Looking sharp as usual."

"Thanks, Irv. Sorry about the drink order thing, I forgot all about your alcoholism."

He looked at me real stern for a moment, then burst out laughing. He put an arm around me and we went inside.

Next, Leanne and Vin came in and I poured their drinks. I offered them both a sip of my own. Leanne declined. Vin took a sip and spat it back at me. "Hell, I never thought something could be both too bitter and too sweet!" I didn't care. Truth is I didn't even give him our best scotch.

Before the meeting, Mom pulled me aside. "When Bill gets here, sit him at the other head of the table."

"But that's Dad's seat."

"I know, sit him down there."

"Okay."

When Bill arrived, he was fidgeting and sweating through his shirt.

"Evening, Nixon," I greeted.

"Shut up. Do you know what the hell this meeting's about? Mom hasn't said a thing to me."

"I don't know Bill, but Mom says to sit in Dad's seat."

"Dad's seat? Why?"

"I don't know. Some sort of surprise or something."

Bill took the seat at the head of the table. Mom appeared from behind the heavy, oak doors. Lucy was by her side. They walked in and Lucy took the seat next to Mom. I looked over at Bill. You could tell his brain was running through every possible scenario that led to this moment. As his shoulders slumped and his cheeks hollowed, he put it together.

We sat in silence until Big Al handed Mom a folder. She began taking out photos and handed the first one to me. In it was Bill, his hand on the hips of a well-built young woman who donned a red dress that hugged her smooth, olive skin. The two of them were leaning in close at what looked like a hotel bar. The accompanying receipts showed that he'd used a company card for drinks, dinner, and a hotel room. I flipped through the next few photos. It was more of Bill and the same woman, each a little more sordid than the last.

Bill peeked over. "What the fuck?" He leaped from his seat.

"You sit right down!" Mom hollered.

Bill retreated. "Luce, let me explain. Look, this is hardly the place for this…"

"Bill," said Mom, "this is a family meeting. The agenda for tonight is discussing the punishment for your betrayal of this family. This is *exactly* the place for it."

"Betrayal?" He forced a laugh. "C'mon, Mom."

Her face was stone. "How long has it been with this woman, Bill? A few years? What have you been telling her?" Her usually firm voice wavered at the implication of her questions. "You know exactly what loose lips can cause in our line of work. And your *father* paid the price for it."

Bill shook his head. "You can't put that shit on me. You're crazy, Mom. I won't even–" He couldn't bring himself to think the thought and turned to his wife. She didn't look back. "Look, Luce, if I could talk to you alone, I can explain all this."

"No. I've spoken to Mom, and we decided together that this

is the best way to deal with it." Lucy's voice quivered. Big Al handed her a tissue as a few tears trickled down her cheek.

I looked around the room. Part of me wanted to smile. Another part saw Lucy and thought of the kids and felt ashamed. The oaf from high school, bones splintering on the goal post, wailed in my ear.

"Bill, as my oldest son, I've tried to instill in you the values of duty, loyalty, and family. That's what this business is based on. That's all there is left when you tear everything else away. Lucy is our family. By betraying her, you've betrayed us all. I wanted you to sit in that chair and think about your father, and how you've spat on everything he ever stood for."

At that, Lucy began to sob. Bill tried running over to her, but Big Al intercepted him. Leanne went over and embraced her instead.

"Get off me you piece of shit!" Bill yelled. He stormed into the kitchen. I looked at Mom. She nodded in the direction of the kitchen so I went in after him.

"Look, Joe, you gotta help me out here," he babbled. "Look, this is crazy. This is all a big misunderstanding. You gotta help me convince Mom this is a big misunderstanding, so I can talk to Lucy alone. And that shit about how this might relate to Dad? C'mon, Joe."

I paused for a moment. I wasn't sure what to say. "You need a drink, Bill. We'll get this all straightened out."

"A drink? Fine, fine. Hell, I could use one."

"Great, what'll it be?"

"And to think, Mom had her thugs following me around? Spying on me? Is that what we call good family values?"

"I'm having a Boulevardier, I could fix you one."

"Sure."

"You want that with rye or bourbon?"

"What?"

"Some people like it better with rye. I sure do."

Bill grabbed me and shook me good. "Listen, Joe, you gotta understand, this is my marriage we're talking about, you're my brother, you gotta help me!" He paused. "You don't think Mom will hurt her, do you?"

"Your girlfriend?" I chuckled. I couldn't help it. It was amusing to watch Bill pal up to me. Funny how that happened when I was the last one left.

"You wouldn't get it," he snarled. "You never got anything. You're real fucked in the head you know that? You always have been." He simmered with brutish frustration and coiled like he was going to hit me, but thought better of it. I didn't say a word.

Mom called us in from the dining room. She had a phone in front of her. "P.J.," she said, "phone my attorney, Mr. Printz."

"What, you going to sue me, Mom?" Bill rolled his eyes.

Mom held the phone up to her ear. "Mr. Printz? Hi, it's Mrs. Gray…Yes, about the matter we spoke on earlier. Well, I need to come into the office early tomorrow morning on important business regarding my will. I'd like to discuss some alterations…A what?… Yes, a codicil, I suppose. You lawyers and your fancy words. Anyhow, I'll see you tomorrow."

She hung up.

"What, you're going to leave it all to him?" Bill shot me a look. "What the hell's he going to do with it? Open a bar?"

Mom stared at Bill. "Why not? A bar could be good for business. Now get the hell out of here."

Lucy was still crying as Leanne held her.

P.J. took a stack of papers from in front of Lucy and brought them over to Bill.

Bill left like a hurricane.

I took a sip of my drink and tried not to smile.

THE EVENING DRAGGED on like the secondhand was stuck in molasses. No one heard from Bill after the meeting and Mom made up the guest room for Lucy. Leanne went over to Bill and Lucy's house to watch the kids. I figured I'd wait a day or two to let things settle before following up about the bar.

The night didn't provide any solace or rest. I sat up thinking over the fall out of the evening's events. Was Mom bluffing? Would she exile Bill from the family business and cut him out of the will? Besides the bar, what would that mean for me? I went down and had a drink. As the sting of the whiskey, chased by bittersweetness, settled my thoughts, I saw a figure through the back window. It was a woman emerging from the trees and coming towards the house. I put on my jacket and went out to the back porch and saw that it was Lucy. I hustled out to her. She wore a nightgown and slippers that crunched the frost-coated lawn. She floated towards me like an apparition.

"Lucy, what're you doing out this late? It's cold as hell out here." My spine itched and my extremities felt like icicles — and it wasn't just the frigid air. Scarring her soft features were lines of vile righteousness. The blood in her face refused to hide from the cold.

I put my hands on her shoulders. "Let's get inside." I ushered her towards the house. Then, from the depths of the property, the sting of metal on stone screeched through the crooked trees. Lucy's face twitched with satisfaction.

"You were always the good one," she breathed, as her frozen hand brushed against my cheek. She continued towards the house.

I followed the path through the trees to the graveyard, an intermittent clang my beacon in the dark. As I neared the edge of the patch of trees, I saw a small headlight illuminating gravestones. I emerged and saw P.J. and Big Al digging in Dad's empty grave. Every few swings, P.J.'s shovel nicked the corner of Great Aunt Sheila's adjacent headstone. Next to them was a rolled-up tarp, leaking. A wave of dark, silk hair spilled from one end.

"Is that—" I stammered. "And Dad's—" I couldn't get anything out.

The two men looked at me before exchanging glances. P.J. put the shovel down and stepped forward. "Look, Joe, you don't have to be a part of this. You should go inside."

"You killed her?" I spat. "You killed her and you're burying her in Dad's grave?" My chest stung like my lungs were wrapped in barbed wire.

"It's what your Mom and Lucy decided."

I tried to control my breathing but it came in turbulent bursts. I launched towards P.J. Big Al intercepted me — saving me the embarrassment of what I'd do if I'd made it to him. He squeezed me as I tried to wriggle free. My head was buried in his massive chest and the slow rhythm of his heart calmed me a bit. He sensed it and let me go. I was close enough to see down into the hole; spurs of bone peeked through the soil.

"Sorry you had to see it, Joe," P.J. said, as if I'd caught them shoplifting. He glanced at his phone. "Your Mom's inside, she wants a word."

MOM WAS WAITING on a couch in the living room. I took a seat across. I felt my lip quiver and moisture was pressing at the corners of my eyes but I fought like hell not to let it squeeze through.

She sighed. "I'm sorry about all the secrecy, Joseph. Please know it's because I want to shield you from some of the things we do. I know it doesn't—fit you."

I looked down at my trembling hands. I folded them and they held each other still. "Dad's grave…"

"Understand that your father's grave is for other purposes. It's for people who may have played a role in his death. I find it poetic." Her voice was filled with conviction. "Besides, people don't look for people in other people's graves."

"But she didn't do anything…"

"Oh? And you know that how? When I got word of how long Bill has been seeing that woman, I knew there was a chance she could be the source of information that allowed our enemies to track your father's whereabouts and seize an opportunity."

"You got proof, Mom?"

Her eyes shifted. "Not firm proof, no. It's more conjectural. But that wasn't her only crime."

"The other crime was Bill's crime. And the punishment doesn't fit. Hell, Mom, you *killed* her for having an affair with Bill."

She raised an eyebrow. "Oh, I didn't decide to kill her. Lucy needed to make the final call. I interrogated the woman regarding whether she passed on any information that put your father at risk, but the poor girl couldn't get a word out.

I offered her life for information. She kept sobbing. But Lucy made the call on whether to dispose of her."

I thought of the rotting bones and guts and tissues a layer deeper and was struck by an eerie cognizance of the death around me. The knots of right and wrong unraveled and I felt in me, firmly, for once, how they should be sorted.

"There won't be anything like that in my bar."

"Pardon?"

"My bar, Mom. It's not going to be some front for your crimes. It's going to be for serving drinks. And I make the final calls there." My face was wet and I tasted salt at the corners of my lips.

She looked at me with restrained pride. "All right, Joseph. Deal. How about a drink?"

I sniffed and nodded and went to the bar cart.

"I'll have a—"

"I'm making Boulevardiers."

**Nils Gilbertson** is a crime and mystery fiction writer and practicing attorney. A San Francisco Bay Area native, Nils currently resides in our nation's capital, where he spends his time avoiding politicians. His short stories have appeared in *Mystery Weekly*, *Pulp Modern*, *Pulp Adventures*, *Close to the Bone*, and *Thriller Magazine*. You can reach him at nilspgilbertson@gmail.com and find him on Twitter @NilsGilbertson.

## Pulp Modern
## Tech Noir Special Edition

Tom Barlow • C.W. Blackwell
Deborah L. Davitt
Angelique Fawns • Nils Gilberton
J.D. Graves • Zakariah Johnson
Jo Perry • Don Stoll

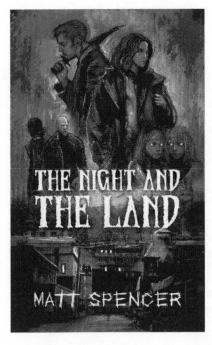
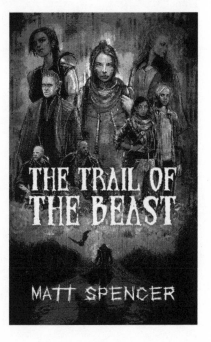

# "Bold, Action-Packed Storytelling"

—John Daker, Amazon.com

## Contact
Get the latest news and announcements at <pulp-modern.blogspot> and <facebook.com/pulpmodern> Post feedback on Facebook or write to <pulpmodern@yahoo.com>

## Links
Timothy Friend <timothyfriend.net>
Adam S. Furman <adamsfurman.com>
Nils Gilbertson <twitter.com/NilsGilbertson>
Peter W.J. Hayes <peterwjhayes.com>
Serena Jayne <serenajayne.com>
Mandi Jourdan <Twitter.com/@MandiJourdan>
Ran Scott <Twitter.com/@RSPMystery>
Bob Vojtko <facebook.com/bob.vojtko.7>
Victoria Weisfeld <vweisfeld.com>

Get a free ebook of *The Digest Enthusiast* book one on Magzter when you sign up for the Larque Press mailing list. More info at <LarquePress.com> For a weekly dose of digest magazine news and history visit the News Digest blog at <LarquePress.com>

## Advertisers' Index

Manufactured by Amazon.ca
Bolton, ON

28087306R10079